VENGEANCE

Robert Crutchfield

ISBN: 0615429521
ISBN-13: 9780615429526

Library of Congress Control Number: 2010943067

Vengeance, Sierra Vista, Arizona

Thank you

So many people helped in the making of Vengeance. I'd like to thank my wife Adrianne for staying up late nights with me editing so many times. Thank you Jeff for helping me add a voice to the characters that desperately needed it. Thank you Dad for helping me push this project to the next level. Thank you very much Jared and Jessica Stevens for putting up with my infatuation with commas and your editing prowess (Dante Gibson...enough said). To my various critics, thank you for being blunt and honest. Without your honesty, this book would have been an epic failure. Thank you to my daughters, to whom I owe the most gratitude. Without having them as inspiration, Vengeance would be a dull and lifeless book. Thank you to my all my friends and family who helped promote this book without ever having read it. You are all amazing and I don't know what I'd do without you. Thank you to the soldiers and veterans of the armed services. My time with you has allowed this book to spring from war memoir to fictional work of art. Lastly, I'd like to reiterate my gratitude to my wife. You know how much this project means to me and you stood by side to make it happen. You never let me quit or give up. You are amazing, wonderful, and spectacular all at the same time.

Prologue

The image on the flat screen television hesitates, skipping even though the television is brand new. It is evident that this family DVD has been played to the point of exhaustion. The dim room is silent except for the sounds of splashing and juvenile joy on the screen. The three children in the video are playing in a backyard swimming pool.

The lone boy who is twelve years old pats his stomach and belches loudly into the camera. He gives a toothy grin and with a running start launches himself into the water. The cannonball he performs causes a mighty splash.

"Hey!" An amused female voice shouts. "You almost got water on your dad's new camera."

The camera pans to a man tending to a barbeque grill. "Hi, honey!" The woman's voice calls.

The man looks up from the grill and smiles broadly. A little girl no older than five sprints into view, dripping wet and giggling. She smashes head-long into the man's leg. He stumbles slightly and laughs as his youngest daughter hugs his leg. "I love you daddy!" As quickly as she had arrived she runs back to the pool and all the fun.

"So, what are you making for your family, 'Chef'?" The woman behind the camera inquires.

"The usual. My famous spice-rubbed ribs for you, Brian and Jenny. Oh, and big fat New York strip steaks for Katie and I." He winks and points off camera.

The camera follows his finger to where their oldest daughter stretched out on a beach towel in the grass, sunbathing and texting on her cell phone simultaneously.

"That better not be a boy that you're texting, young lady!" The father's voice jokes off camera.

The eleven year old girl looks up and slides her sun glasses down her nose. She smiles slyly, rolling her eyes and goes right back to texting.

Crimson tears cascade down the cheeks of the man watching the DVD. Unable to bear anymore, Jayden Endsley chokes back the rest of his tears and smears his face scarlet trying to wipe the blood away. He sighs audibly, completely emotionally and physically drained. He turns off the DVD and trudges from the room.

It takes all of his energy to climb his stairs towards his bedroom. Family photos line the walls of the stairway. His shattered family stares back at him with smiling faces; smiling faces at the aquarium, smiling faces at the zoo. Memories of birthdays, Christmas and school plays. He closes his eyes tightly as he climbs, haunted by what was lost to him forever.

On top of that, Jayden thirsts. His unnourished body protests every step up the stairs. He ignores the gnawing hunger, focused only on the nightmares that awaited him once he slumbered. He knows that without sustenance his unconscious mind will take him back to that ghastly night where he had almost lost everything. Jayden doesn't care. He welcomes the terror. He seeks the pain out. These nightmares are his only chance at finding clues.

By the time Jayden reaches the second floor landing, dizziness threatens to overwhelm him. He stumbles, using his hand on the wall for balance. As Jayden struggles to his bedroom, he glances towards his daughter's bedroom, taking solace in it. Katie's was a typical teenage girl's room despite everything that had happened. The latest pop sensation's posters covered her walls. Her bed was a tangled mess of stuffed animals and disheveled blankets. That room is still occupied, but he tries his best to ignore the closed doors to the two empty bedrooms.

He wobbles through the doors of the master bedroom, his head swimming and his vision narrowing. He finally collapses onto the floor. The room spins and lurches sickeningly. He attempts to drag himself to the bed, but can't move another inch. Shuddering, he braces for the coming tumult. His last thoughts before losing himself to the nightmare are of the DVD he watches every night.

* * *

The doors to the theater open and a flock of girls pours into the lobby. A blonde in the midst of a pack of pre-teens exclaims, "I just loved the way that their skin sparkled in the sun!"

Her short, chunky friend next to her is just as excited. "And the way they eat animals instead of humans!"

A pretty brunette in the group chimes in. "It was just so romantic!"

Katie rolls her eyes and turns to her mother as they stride along. "Can you believe that movie? It was completely unrealistic. The lead chick was such a crappy actor too…"

Aaliyah just shakes her head. "You do realize that it was a romance, don't you? It wasn't a documentary about vampires. You should know better than anyone that pop culture doesn't have the slightest idea about what we are."

"It's just so annoying!"

"I know; you constantly reminded me throughout the whole movie. And, I am sorry to interrupt your critique of that mediocre film Katie, but I need you to text your father. Let him know we're on our way."

Katie's fingers fly over the keypad. Her aptitude to text at light speed was an ability that she had acquired long before becoming a vampire. In the five minutes it took for them to walk to the car, Jayden had yet to respond to his daughter. "He never takes this long to get back to me, Mom."

"Call him," Aaliyah instructed as they climbed into the car. "If he doesn't answer, something's wrong."

Jayden's phone goes straight to voicemail. Katie and her mother exchange terrified glances. Aaliyah slams on the gas and they speed towards their suburban sanctuary swerving through traffic.

After some truly tense moments they screech to an abrupt halt in their driveway. Aaliyah had barely thrown the car in park before both girls were rushing towards the front door. She quickly unlocks the door and Katie follows swiftly on her heels. The ear-piercing screams coming from upstairs confirm her fears.

Chapter 1

Jayden wiped the sweat from his brow. "Wrap your leg," he shouted to Aaliyah. Aaliyah was competing for first place in the Las Vegas Jiu Jitsu Championship. She was fighting in the women's one hundred and thirty pound division and losing. When the bell signaling the end of the second period rang, Aaliyah rolled from beneath her stronger opponent and stormed toward her corner and her husband. "I don't need your advice out there" she snarled as she grabbed the towel he held out.

"Well you need somebody's advice; your opponent is destroying you out there." Jayden shot back.

"I've been doing this longer than you, and the only reason you're here is because the instructor is with his son," Aaliyah snapped as she grabbed her bottle of water and began to drink.

"I love you too, honey," Jayden replied sarcastically. He paused for a beat and changed angles. "Listen babe, this girl is much stronger than you."

Aaliyah threw her water bottle to the floor and shot a cutting glance at Jayden. "So what if this cow is stronger; I can still take her."

Jayden grabbed his wife's hand and looked straight into her eyes. "Sweetheart, you have better technique than she does. You can beat her. But you need to use her strength against her." Jayden looked past his wife at her opponent. Although her opponent was in the same one hundred and thirty pound weight division as Aaliyah, she was built like a freight train. Her long, kinky brown hair was tied back in a ponytail. The woman appeared to be staring back at Jayden as she held her hands on her knees, struggling for air while her corner man gave her instructions. "Maybe you could try to lure her in, let her take you down. Just keep your legs around her. She's already winded, so once she tires completely, make your move. If you keep trying to wrestle with her, she is going to win."

Aaliyah loved her husband very much, but she was also a very strong willed and prideful woman who intended to follow her own game plan. With their children in attendance, she wanted to win on her own terms. Her seventeen-year old son, Brian, had taken gold in the young men's one hundred seventy five pound division earlier in the day. Her sixteen-year old daughter, Katie, had placed third in the young women's one hundred fifteen pound division. Even her ten-year-old daughter, Jenny, had a gold medal in the children's division. As far as Aaliyah was concerned, she was the anchor of this family in martial arts. She had been doing it years before she met Jayden, and had insisted that a family that fights together stays together.

Aaliyah adjusted her *gi*, put her mouth guard in, and stared intently at her opponent. She walked to the center of the mat and shook hands with her opponent. The noise from the crowd was deafening, and she could feel Jayden staring at her from behind. *She is incredibly sexy,* he thought as he checked out his wife. Aaliyah was 5'5" and weighed one hundred thirty well-proportioned pounds, with her Italian heritage more-than-evident in her hair and her attitude. Jayden regularly referred to her as his "hot mama". Strangers and friends always asked who did her boobs, and she would always look uncomfortable when answering, "They're real". More than any other physical attribute though, Jayden loved how stunning her eyes were. They were such a pale blue with just a hint of green. She rarely wore make up, and was usually the prettiest woman in the room.

When the buzzer sounded to signal the start of the round, she dove at her opponent's legs trying to tackle her. The stronger woman sprawled backward, kicking her feet behind her and driving her hips down and into Aaliyah's head. Aaliyah tried desperately to free herself, but the woman smashed her harder into the mat. Once Aaliyah's grip was completely broken, the woman spun, repositioned herself and slipped her legs around Aaliyah to immobilize her. Aaliyah couldn't buck the stronger fighter off. As Aaliyah struggled, her opponent began to slide her arms under Aaliyah's jaw like a python. Aaliyah could feel the choke coming but could do nothing to stop it. As the woman flexed her unusually large arms, Aaliyah's vision began to fade. She refused to tap and admit defeat. The last thing she saw before she blacked out was the crowd cheering and her tight-lipped husband in the corner.

As the Endsley vehicle pulled out of the parking lot, Aaliyah kept her eyes closed. She pulled the silver medal from her neck and let it fall to the floor. Jayden knew better than to try to comfort her; it would be the same as saying, *I told you so.* Jenny sat in the back of the SUV between her brother and sister. She picked up her medal and showed Brian for the third time.

"See what I won?" she asked proudly.

Brian laughed and plucked it from her little fingers to examine it. "What an amazing job, baby sis. You kicked some serious butt out there." He pulled his gold medal from around his neck. "Maybe one day you'll win one like this."

Jenny reached for Brian's medal and pulled it over her head. "Yours is super shiny. Is it real gold? Like, pirate's gold?" she asked innocently.

Brian reached between his feet into his gym bag and pulled out a t-shirt and fashioned it around Jenny's head like a pirate bandana. "That's right, Sis. Just like pirate gold. Want to go on an adventure when we get home? I'll make a ship out of pillows and we can act like we are on the high seas."

"I don't think so— I spent two hours cleaning the house last night. You are not going to destroy the living room when we get home. Besides, we have guests coming over for dinner," Aaliyah spoke for the first time since they got into the car.

"Ah, come on Mom. It's just James and Ronin. Have you ever been to their house? A hurricane leaves less clutter in its path than they leave in their house," Brian retorted.

"I'd rather not have our house in complete disarray when we have guests, regardless of who is coming over."

"I have an idea," Jayden interjected. "How about because you all did so well at the tournament, and Mom doesn't want the house to get too messy, why don't we go to Red Lobster?"

Aaliyah pouted and said, "Well at least you and the kids got gold. I'll call Ronin and tell him to meet us at the restaurant for dinner."

All the kids cheered except Katie. "Dad, this is so unfair. You said you would let me practice driving after the tournament," she whined.

"You will get your practice in this weekend sweet heart I promise. In fact, I know I keep telling you that you can drive and then for some reason or another you don't. Let me make it up to you. You can drive us to the mall and I will let you pick out a new outfit then you can drive us home. We can bring Jenny too. It has been too long since our last daddy daughter date." Jayden said convincingly.

Katie crossed her arms and sat back with a smile on her face, not wanting to let on she'd relent. "Well, I suppose that'll work."

As the family piled out of the SUV, Aaliyah stopped Jenny. "Hold on sweetheart," Aaliyah said. She reached around her neck and unclasped her gold locket. "This was your great-grandmother's, then your grandmother's; then she gave it to me. You really impressed me today, honey. You proved you have the dedication to work for something you want, so now it's yours." She placed the locket around Jenny's neck and kissed her cheek. "Take very good care of this honey," she said as she pulled away.

Jenny looked down with a smile at the locket and ran her little thumbs over the gold heart and said, "I love you, Mommy."

* * *

Jayden's body violently shudders with thirst as he falls into a deeper sleep.

Chapter 2

Jayden didn't know how he had gotten where he was, here on the sidelines of the Nevada State high school championship football game. He was coaching the Valley Vikings versus the Elko Rams. He looked up and down the sideline at his players, and then he gazed out at the players on the field. The athletes were exhausted and in pain, but ready to win the battle that had raged for the better part of an hour. He glanced at the game clock, reading 00:05. Elko had just called for a time out. Jayden adjusted his visor and headset as he looked up at his lifelong best friend Ronin Waddilove standing high above him in the coach's box. Jayden could see Ronin's extended belly as he wiped his forehead in search of the right defense to call. Ronin tugged at his shirt, adjusted his headset and began to speak.

"Man, this team is gonna give me an ulcer!" he said.

"Come on Ronin, give me one more stop. What do you think we should do here?" Jayden questioned nervously.

"I think we should go get a beer," Ronin joked.

"You give me the stopper here and I'll buy you a case," Jayden said smiling.

"Say no more buddy, I'm going to be knee-deep in suds tonight. Big James has been a beast all night, let's turn him loose and blitz these boys."

"Big James" Waddilove was a six foot, two hundred thirty five pound senior middle linebacker and the son of the potbellied man calling the defensive signals. Jayden looked at him, nodding his head approvingly. Jayden looked out at the field and his average-sized son.

"But that leaves Brian in single coverage against Dante," Jayden fretted. Dante Gibson was the best receiver in the state.

Ronin laughed nervously and replied, "If your son is as fast as the scouts claim, it shouldn't be a problem. Besides, he's got your blood in him."

Jayden smiled and said, "Let's do it. What do you wanna call?" James was standing one foot in front of Jayden who had his hand on the senior's face mask when Ronin relayed the play.

Ronin smiled and replied, "Eleven Pinch Crucify, Cover One."

As soon as Ronin gave Jayden the play, he relayed it to the big young football player who turned and sprinted out to the field and the defensive huddle. The crowd was screaming and stomping the bleachers so hard James had to scream to be heard by the players standing only a few feet from him.

"One more time boys, just one more stop and these girls will be going home in second place. Eleven Pinch Crucify, Cover One! Brian— you have man coverage on Dante. If you would bother to stop him for a change, I'd really appreciate it," James smiles as he chides his teammate. Brian jokingly punched James in the chest.

"Ready, break!" the team said in unison as they clapped, broke the huddle, and took their positions. The cheerleaders and bands were whipping the crowd into an uncontrollable frenzy as the Elko Rams offense broke their huddle and lined up for the final play of their high school careers. Jayden turned to the stands, located his family and gave them the thumbs up. Aaliyah, Jenny, and Katie cheered emphatically and looked on as James stalked back and forth behind the defensive line like a caged animal. Katie's heart fluttered with each step James took. She could see the firm muscles of his calves as he stomped. "Let's go Brian!" James shouted as he looked back at Brian.

The combination of cold air and sweat made steam pour out of Brian's helmet. His eyes were focused on the receiver across from him. Dante winked at Brian, as they both knew Dante was headed for the end zone. He was the state's best receiver and had already caught eleven passes– two of them for touchdowns– over Brian tonight. His gloved hands were seemingly unable to drop a pass.

The quarterback took the snap from the center and dropped back to pass. Chaos ensued. James exploded through the offensive line without being touched. The quarterback's eyes widened as he saw James running full speed toward him unblocked. As he turned to evade the beast running his way, a running back stepped up to block James. This was a big mistake; James lowered his shoulder and crushed the undersized player, then stepped on him as he continued his pursuit of the quarterback. Just as James was about to hit the terrified quarterback, the frightened boy pitched the ball toward the end zone.

Dante was running full speed as he looked back and located the floating football. He leaped into the air at the goal line.

When Dante attempted to pull the ball into his body in mid flight, Brian put his helmet into Dante's back and wrapped his arms around him. Brian remembers it as the hardest he had ever hit anyone. At the point of impact he felt the wind escape from Dante. As they crashed to the ground, Brian saw the ball rolling on the ground five feet from him. Brian did not hear a sound as the play was developing but heard plenty of noise while he lay on the ground as the crowd erupted.

Ronin jumped and screamed "Hell, yeah!" as he threw the headset aside. He scrambled to pick up the headset and screamed into the mouth piece "We did it, buddy! I told you we could stomp those scrubs!" He looked at the scoreboard: *Home 20 - Guest 17.*

Brian got to his feet and ran over and hugged his father. "Coach, how'd I look?"

Jayden grabbed his son with tears in his eyes, and yelled, "You were awesome, son! Go celebrate with the guys."

Brian's grin was a mile wide as he ran over to join the jubilation in the middle of the field with his team. Jayden looked into the stands and waved to his wife and daughters who were screaming and jumping. As he surveyed the crowd, his gaze rested on a small group of people at the base of the bleachers, softly clapping and staring right at him.

Chapter 3

After the game, Jayden took his family out for ice cream. They parked across the street on the fifth level of a parking garage and piled out of the vehicle. They headed across the street still ecstatic about the big win, to the ice cream parlor. Aaliyah was walking a few steps behind Jayden and checked out her husband. While still incredibly handsome, she noticed that he had put on a few pounds. Jayden was 6' 3" and weighed two hundred and forty five pounds, a little less symmetrical than when they first met. Back in his prime, he was commonly mistaken for Dwayne Johnson, aka "The Rock". She pictured him with his old 34" waist, and his massive chest and back. He still had the massive chest and back, but with fewer muscles. Jayden was imitating Brian's big tackle as he playfully wrapped his arms around Jenny and scooped her off the ground. He spun his daughter playfully while she was draped over his shoulder. Jenny squealed with laughter as she clung to his shirt. She yelled, "Mommy, Daddy's a silly goober." Aaliyah smiled and pretended to hear what her daughter was saying, but she was actually looking at Jayden's face.

He might be larger, she thought, *but I'm every bit in love with him as the day we met. I couldn't imagine a better father. I mean he definitely had an issue controlling his temper when we were younger, but the kids have softened his heart so much.* A part of her realized that she was more attracted to the father he had become than the young athlete he had once been. A smile came across her face as she lowered her head and continued walking. Jayden reached the door of the ice cream parlor and pulled it open. He placed Jenny on the ground so she could walk. She dizzily stumbled into the restaurant, followed by her siblings. Aaliyah entered behind the children and felt a light tap on her butt. She turned around and gave her husband a dirty look, with a devilish smile. Jayden winked at her and let the door close behind him as he entered. The Endsley family were the only people in the shop besides the young freckle-faced boy behind the counter.

Katie and Brian ordered their ice cream, while Jenny stood on her father's feet. Holding his hands, she kept her balance on his size thirteen shoes. She swayed back and forth singing to him, "I want strawberry ice cream and you get mint chocolate chip, Daddy." Jayden was asking Aaliyah if she had brought her debit card as he had forgotten his in the SUV. Jenny all the while kept up her request. Jayden finally lifted his daughter so they were face to face. With a fake scowl on his face he said, "Alright young lady, you get strawberry, but I want cookies and cream."

"But daddy you always get the green kind after we win."

"I know but this time I want COOKIES!" He buried his head in her neck and gave her as many kisses on her collar bone as he could while she squirmed and laughed uncontrollably. Every few kisses he would take a breath and yell 'cookies' while continuing his kissy monster attack.

The young boy behind the counter scratched his head while the scene in front of him took place. Stealing glances at Katie, he asked them if they wanted anything else. Jayden finally put his daughter down and she rushed into her mother's arms. He laughed and told the young employee, "I will have one scoop of strawberry ice cream, kid's size, and a banana split with three scoops of cookies and cream." Aaliyah gave him a look of malcontent.

"Do you really think you need three scoops coach? You aren't going to be able to go the distance in next month's tournament if you keep eating like this." She patted his belly as she grabbed Jenny's ice cream and walked back to the table.

Jayden waited a few more moments at the counter while his delectable treat was prepared. Once it was ready, he reached for a napkin and spoon and headed over to his family. They were already sitting down and eating.

"…and I knew I couldn't jump as high as him, so I figured I had to hit him with everything I had. I still can't believe we won!"

"I'm so proud of you sweetie," Aaliyah said. "You were spectacular. You were the hero in my book today."

"Let's not forget who coached the team to victory," Jayden said with his mouth full of whipped cream.

"Yes honey, you were good today too," Aaliyah brushed off her husband and kept on speaking. "You and James completely shut down the offense."

"Yeah James was pretty phenomenal. He set a Nevada state record for sacks tonight," Brian replied.

Katie, who had been texting and eating her frozen yogurt, lifted her eyes from her cell phone for a split second. "Yeah, James was definitely the reason we won tonight," she muttered under her breath as she turned her attention back to her vibrating phone.

"Excuse me young lady, your brother did great and might I add, saved the game for the team," Aaliyah retorted.

Swallowing a mouthful of ice cream Jayden interjects, "Also, I coached the team to victory."

"Jayden, we all know you did a great job coaching. I am talking about how well our son played," Aaliyah responded. "And as for you girlie, you need to be nice to your brother."

"Whatever," Katie muttered as she started texting again.

Aaliyah sat there watching her text, her fingers clenching the ice cream spoon tighter. Katie hit the send button, returning a fraction of her attention back to her family.

"Oh Mom before I forget, can I go to the party this weekend?" Katie asked.

"Who's party?"

"Oh it's Laura Billings. You know who she is. You met her mother at parents' night last year."

Brian interrupted, "No way mom. Laura Billings is a skank. She's been with every guy on the wrestling team. Besides, Katie only wants to go to the party because James will be there."

"That's not true Mom. Laura is not a skank. Plus, I am not interested in James. He's way too full of himself."

Brian cut in again, "And you are full of sh..."

"Watch your mouth young man," Aaliyah chastised her son. She looked at her husband who was still shoveling ice cream in his mouth. "What do you think Jayden?"

Jayden glanced up from his meal to see his family staring at him. Wiping the ice cream from his shirt, he tried to catch up to the conversation. "What do I think about what honey?"

"Should Katie be allowed to go to a party this weekend?"

"Um, I thought we were going camping?" The table stayed quiet so Jayden continued. "I guess it's not a big deal though. I need to clean the garage anyway. Wait, is Brian going?"

Brian stated matter-of-factly, "No way dad. I am taking Jessica out to Lake Mead this weekend. You said I could use the boat."

"Hmm, I suppose I did. If you wreck my boat I will smash you." Jayden winked at his first born. He was starting to become a softy in his old age. "Who's party is it anyway, Katie?"

"It's Laura Billings' party, Daddy" she said exasperated.

"I don't know, I heard she's kind of a skank," Jayden said.

Brian almost fell out of his chair laughing.

"What? I teach weight training and the guys talk," Jayden said.

Brian suddenly shouted out in pain. He winced, and grabbed his bruised leg under the table. Katie glared at her brother, threatening to kick him again.

"You're such a douche bag," Katie scowled at her brother.

He smiled back at his sister. "Don't you have to text your B.F.F. and tell her you won't be at that party?"

She held her hand under the table beyond the vision of her parents, but where her brother could still see; flipping him off. He openly blew her a spiteful kiss in return.

"Knock it off you two," Jayden said. He felt his baby girl's head slump in exhaustion on his lap. He softly stroked her hair. "It's way past Jenny's bedtime. We need to get her home."

Aaliyah patted her husband's arm.

"Take Brian and Jenny to the car, I'm going to have a talk with our daughter."

"Okay babe, take your time; Jenny's already out cold." He looked up at Brian who was already on his feet and picking Jenny up. Jayden slipped out of the booth and opened the door for Brian.

Katie looked up oblivious to what was happening. She had been pounding her thumbs across the smart phone screen. She figured it was time to leave and started to stand up.

"Sit down!" Aaliyah shouted a little too loud. The boy behind the counter perked up. Aaliyah shot him a fierce glance and he retreated to the back of the kitchen. "What the hell is wrong with you Katie? When have I ever allowed you to treat your brother like that? This is his special night and it seems like you are trying to ruin it for him."

"That's not fair mom. He's such a jerk to me and you never yell at him."

"Please," Aaliyah shot back. "I have smacked your brother more times than I have ever even yelled at you. You are addicted to that cell phone, and there will be some new rules for it. You will not use it at dinner, or anytime the family is together."

"Come on mom…"

"I don't want to hear it Katie."

Katie looked at the table and a tear escaped her eye. Aaliyah took a deep breath and started again, this time more calmly.

"Honey, your brother is going to college in a few months and who knows when we will see him again? The time we spend as a family now is very important. I know your father seems to spend more time with Jenny and Brian, but it's not because he doesn't love you as much. He coaches Brian's team, and Jenny is his little Jiu Jitsu protégé. He coached your softball team, but you didn't want to play this year, remember? He and I love you so much honey. I have been so consumed with work lately and I know we haven't spent nearly enough time together." Aaliyah got out of the booth and slid in next to her. She put her arm around her daughter and pulled her in close for a hug. She held on to Katie for a moment more. As they separated Aaliyah smiled at her daughter and wiped her tears. "Hey, let me talk to your father. There's no reason you shouldn't go to that party. I know you're a responsible young woman and you will do what is right."

Katie smiled at her mom and gave her another hug. The women got out of the booth and Katie reached for her purse.

"I need to freshen myself up mom."

"I need to use the bathroom too."

The women looked around for the restrooms only to see that there was only one.

Aaliyah let her daughter go first. She pulled out her phone and sent a text message to her husband letting him know that they would still be another couple of minutes. After ten minutes Katie emerged from the restroom looking more refreshed. Aaliyah grabbed her purse and stepped in the restroom letting the door close...

Jayden walked out of the ice cream parlor into the night with Brian and Jenny in tow. Brian adjusted his sleeping sister in him arms as they trekked back to their vehicle. They walked up the block and crossed the street. As they headed across the parking lot, toward the parking structure, a black Suburban swerved into the parking lot and skidded to a stop directly in front of them.

The group of Goths who had caught Jayden's eye in the bleachers at the game stepped out of the large

SUV. Rock music was blaring from the vehicle as the occupants exited.

The first one out of the vehicle was the driver, Pagan. Pagan was a mountain of a man who stood 6'9" and weighed three hundred and sixty five pounds. His short, cropped black hair accentuated his large head, but he didn't need a thing to accentuate his massive biceps and powerful legs. His skin was tightly stretched over his frame and his large nose and lips seemed to fit his overgrown goatee. Next to exit the truck were a set of gorgeous women, Natalie and Alexis. They stepped out at the same time from the back seat; Jayden stared at them as much for how they were dressed as he did for how they were built. These Amazonian women were extremely good looking and they both had bodies that he was sure were manufactured in a plastic surgeon's office. Natalie's bleach blonde hair extended down to the middle of her back, which swayed as she walked. Alexis had straight black hair that billowed in the wind. She brushed it out of her almond shaped eyes as she fell in step with her counterpart. Jayden and Brian gawked at the tight "boy shorts," six inch stilettos and halter tops. The minimal thread in their tops restrained two pair of the most perfect double D's they had ever seen, but this was Vegas and the girls were dressed to kill. The last to exit was a modestly tall man named Drake. He had shoulder length, curly black hair and appeared to be Mediterranean. With dashing good looks and thin facial features, he appeared to be the leader of this crew. Drake took in his surroundings as he stepped out of the truck. His plain white tee shirt clung to his chiseled torso. He bent over for a moment and dusted off his tattered jeans. His silver crucifix caught the moonlight as he closed the car door. The foursome began to walk towards Jayden and his children, led by Drake with the sexy twins next and Pagan bringing up the rear. Their movements were fluid and determined as they walked, as if they were moving in slow motion. As the group got closer Jayden could see that Drake's eyes were black as night. They were completely opaque. In fact, it seemed as though the black of his pupils were swishing into the whites of his eyes as merlot swishes in a wine glass. His fingernails were filed to a point and painted black. Although it wasn't cold enough to be wearing one, Drake had on a long black trench coat that almost touched the ground. Even from where Jayden stood, he could tell the man's flesh was smooth and flawless.

Pagan was drinking from the largest bottle of Patron that Jayden had ever seen. He appeared to be kissing the neck of one of the girls in front of him before he took a swig of alcohol. It wasn't until they were just outside of arm's reach that Jayden realized the man was actually biting her neck and swishing her blood in his mouth with the tequila. The group stopped two feet from the Endsleys. Jayden instinctively pulled his kids behind him.

"Out for a walk with the family after the big win, Coach?" Drake asked.

Jayden turned and looked behind him for Aaliyah and Katie; they were nowhere to be seen. Jayden had been in bad situations before, but this seemed different; almost eerie, these people didn't look normal. The dim lighting seemed to play tricks on his eyes, because these people looked otherworldly. The thugs, Jayden could now see, all had liquid pupils that seemed to swish into the whites of their eyes. Jayden tried his best to put his fear in check and not let his mind play tricks on him. He had seen one too many horror movies, he thought. They had to be human, he reasoned with himself, because what he thought he saw didn't exist. Once he had reasoned himself calm enough to speak, Jayden said, "Look guys, we don't want any problems."

Pagan stopped drinking and smiled big enough to display his half inch long razor-sharp fangs.

"Come on Drake, let's finish these guys off quick and go find their bitches." Pagan said, gesturing towards the upper levels of the parking structure.

Jayden flushed red with fury and chose his next words carefully because he was sure a fight was imminent, but he had to try and talk his way out of this horrible mess. *"I don't know what you want, but if you touch my family, I'll break every bone in your body and choke the life out of you,"* Jayden thought. Drake smiled broadly as he ran his fingers through his curly long hair.

"You assume breathing and life are connected I presume?" Drake asked as he turned his head slightly and stared hard at Jayden.

Jayden's eyes grew wide as if he had seen a ghost; this man had just read his mind.

Brian held his sister tighter, moved even closer to his father and said, "Come on guys, please! We don't have any money."

"Money?" Drake inquired coldly. "No boy, I didn't come for something so provincial. I've come for my stolen property. I've come for my book," he added.

Jayden was shaking his head side-to-side when he inquired, "What the hell are you talking about? You plan on mugging me over a stupid book? I genuinely don't know what you are talking about. But I will get whatever book you are talking about and you can have it. Just please leave my family alone."

Ignoring the plea, Drake stepped closer to Jayden, who reared back slightly. "You received a book online recently; one that was not that proprietor's to give," Drake replied in a cold monotone voice, only inches from Jayden's ear.

A book? Is this guy serious? He wants to kill me and my family over a book? Jayden thought.

"That's right," Drake said. Again Jayden looked at Drake quizzically, trying to digest the fact that this man was reading his mind.

"Listen guys, I've gotten lots of books online. I don't know what the hell you're talking about, but if you tell me which book I'll give it back to you, no cost."

"Ah, we will get the book, but sadly you won't be around to give it to us," Drake said. "As far as which book, it's called <u>De Aeterna Nox</u>," he added.

Brian looked baffled by the title and glanced at his father, who was still trying to diffuse the situation. Jenny had woken up and was quivering in her brothers arms.

"<u>The Book of Eternal Night</u>?" Jayden said inquisitively, as he thought back to the first email that read "You've won a novel!" "That thing was practically forced on me, now you say it's stolen and you want to kill me for having it?" he shouted after realizing what the strange man in front of him was talking about.

"You wouldn't be trying to play me for a fool, would you Coach?" Drake asked. Jayden stared at Drake a second before he replied.

"Play you? About a goddamn book! I haven't even read it and like I said a website gave me the damned thing. I don't know why you are doing this but if any of you take another step toward my family the big guy is the first to get his jaw broken."

"So you haven't read it, huh?" Drake questioned ignoring the threat. He began shifting his gaze from one family member to the other, nodding his head up and down slowly.

Jayden kept talking as he glanced around the area. He was simply trying to buy time until a security guard made their normal rounds. He racked his mind for an escape plan but these people had blocked his potential run to his vehicle.

"What makes this book so special that you're willing to kill me and my family for it?" Jayden asked nervously.

Without warning, Drake's demeanor suddenly changed. With his eyes ablaze and his lips pulled back, he bared his teeth while he spit the next words at Jayden. From this vantage point Jayden could see Drake's canines had been filed down into razor sharp fangs.

"You insignificant peasant!" Drake exclaimed as he started to circle Jayden and his children. "I've tracked this book for more years than you could comprehend and finally I find it with you!" he added as he continued to circle the frightened group. Jayden turned to look at Drake, who was now behind him. Jayden looked at him as if he were speaking a different language. "I bet you have no concept of what you have, do you?" Drake asked as he stepped in front of Jayden. He was now only inches from Jayden's face. "That book belongs to me and my kind. Our secrets are our own. That book was no work of fiction," Drake spat, slightly increasing his volume while gesturing wildly with his right hand.

Jayden couldn't believe what was happening. This was absolutely ridiculous; this psychopath was really starting to scare him. Jayden's mind raced with what to do, but he did not have time to waste. I can't stand here frozen, just waiting for these things to attack me, he thought. The few people who were in the parking lot were paying no attention to the events that were unfolding. This usually bustling strip mall had only a couple dwindling employees locking up their shops. The security guard wasn't coming and there was no way out. Drake had taken a step back from Jayden, but he still had his liquid eyes locked on him. Jayden balled his fist and stepped forward for maximum power. Then he swung his right hand at Drake with everything he had. His fist collided with Drake's jaw; Jayden heard bones shattering … only they were the bones in his hand. He yelled and grimaced in pain as he shook his right hand, trying to alleviate the pain. He looked up from his aching hand and saw Drake who was now grinning cynically at him. Jayden's mind was full of fear when he tried to elbow Drake in the throat, only to miss. Drake grabbed Jayden by the throat and with minimum effort tossed him thirty feet into the glass of the valet attendant's booth, knocking him out cold.

"Dad!" Brian screamed as he turned and sprinted away with Jenny in his arms. He took four steps before Pagan clothes-lined him.

Brian's feet came off the ground and his sister went flying to the earth. She began to scream loudly as she landed.

"Son of a bitch," Brian said as he blinked hard trying to regain focus while attempting to get to his feet.

"Hmm, Pagan will suffice," the big man said as he bent down and lifted Brian up by his hair until his feet were off the ground. Jenny was still sobbing when she stood up and ran over to help her father.

Pagan clasped his giant hand around Brian's neck, immobilizing him in the air. Alexis and Natalie sauntered in around the helpless boy. Brian tried to look down and see what was happening,

but the hand around his throat kept his face to the sky. Alexis ran her finger tips across the zipper of Brian's shorts as she stepped behind him. Natalie gently caressed Brian's face and let her shimmering black finger nails slide down his neck softly scraping the boy's tender flesh. Alexis clutched Brian's member in her palm and began stimulating the terrified teenager. Natalie rubbed her breasts along Brian's chest. Against his will, Brian's blood began flowing to his genitals. Then, without any preamble, Alexis ripped Brian's penis from his body, causing an endless geyser of blood to gush out. Natalie dug her claws into the star athlete's chest and ripped his pectoral muscle from the right side of his chest. As Brian dangled barely alive from Pagan's death grip, the creatures began feasting on him.

Jenny was cautiously stepping through the broken glass to get to her father. She started crying hysterically and shaking her father.

"Daddy, you gotta wake up and help Brian," she screamed at Jayden.

Jayden was concussed and had a hard time getting his bearing. He rolled over into the fetal position waiting for the ringing in his ears to subside. He could barely acknowledge that Jenny was trying to get his attention. He placed his hands on the ground to aid in his standing only to feel his broken right hand give way. He slid his knees underneath himself and used his good hand to hold him steady while he climbed to his feet. Jayden looked up just in time to see his firstborn child have his entire throat ripped out. Blood spouted out of his neck, while all four creatures devoured the remaining blood in his body. Jayden bent down and picked up a shard of broken glass in his left hand. Noticing that the creatures weren't watching him at all, he grabbed Jenny and laid her amongst the rubble. He grabbed the broken wood shards and concealed her from view. She winced as a piece of glass cut into her. Jayden told her to be strong and stumbled past Jenny, closing the distance between himself and his son. As he stalked an unsuspecting Drake, he swung the primitive weapon at Drake's throat. The glass struck Drakes throat, but didn't even scratch him. The strange and sickening thing was that Drake was so preoccupied with drinking Brian's blood, that he didn't even notice Jayden's attempt to slit his throat. Jayden could see Pagan was crushing what little bit of life was left in his son. Jayden jumped on Pagan's back and tried to stab his eye. Pagan easily shrugged Jayden off of his back causing him to fall to the floor. As he hit the ground, Pagan lifted his foot in the air and with a deafening crunch brought it down on Jayden's femur. Jayden cried out as his leg was crushed. He could feel the shards of smashed bone moving around as Pagan ground his foot into Jayden's leg for good measure. Tears were streaming down Jayden's face not because of the pain racking his body, but because he knew his son was dying and there was no way to stop it. As Jayden lay there in agony, he peered through the gory melee and his eyes locked with his son's. Brian was almost dead, but he mouthed the words "I love you dad". Jayden reached over and picked up the glass shard, attempting in vain to roll over and slice Pagans Achilles tendon. The attempt was futile. Pagan instead kicked Jayden in the mouth, busting several of his teeth out. His whole head was ringing as the buzzing in his ears made him all but deaf.

Reeling from the kick, Jayden's mind was racing and fear had overcome him. The only thing he could think of was his daughter. With his mouth full of blood, he screamed for Jenny to run.

Jenny realized that in order to get to her mother she would have to pass the gaze of the creatures. Jenny sprinted toward the ramp leading to the upper floors of the parking garage. She was overcome with fear and couldn't stop crying, but she continued to run hard. Breathing heavily, Jenny looked back over her shoulder as she rounded the ramp to the second floor.

"Mommy," she cried as she surveyed the building, but she didn't see anyone. She thought for a moment before she came up with the idea of hiding. She crawled underneath a large pickup truck. The structure was eerily quiet as she waited under the truck, which was not good because she continued to see her brother being mauled in her mind. She tried to shake the images as she debated whether or not to come out of her hiding place and try to locate her mother. She tried to stay quiet, but the images in her head were causing her to whimper. She had finally decided to go and look for her mother when she felt a hand on her ankle. Drake had reached under the truck and yanked her from the undercarriage. The little girl dangled upside down a few feet off the ground, but she could see that she was firmly in the clutches of Drake. He was staring into the little girl's eyes as her brother's blood dripped from his hands and face. Grabbing her shirt he turned her right side up so they were eye to eye. He seemed mesmerized as he gently stroked her face. She tried to scream, the high pitch adolescent scream of little girls, when Drake slammed her into the side of the vehicle. Knocking the wind from her lungs he quietly asked her to be quiet. He saw the glistening locket around her neck. He ripped it off of her and placed it in his pocket.

"Let her go!" Jayden screamed from far behind Drake. He was bleeding and crawling up the ramp. As he pulled himself up the ramp on his elbows, Pagan and the females were behind him, kicking him every couple of steps. From twenty feet away, Jayden stared at his little girl as Drake bared his fangs and dug his teeth deep into her neck. Jayden had only drug himself a few feet before Drake removed her lifeless body from his mouth and stared right at Jayden. Then Drake threw his head back and let out a roar of dominance so loud it set off car alarms in the structure. Jayden reached out to his baby girl, blood pouring from his own mouth. Drake then looked back at Jenny and proceeded to rip her head off with her spine still attached. He grabbed the spine and let the head trail behind on the floor.

Pagan grabbed Jayden's broken leg and drug him toward the bottom of the car garage. Whistling a lullaby, Drake walked past Jayden and tossed Jenny's head on the hood of a nearby car. A scream pierced Jayden's ears until he realized it wasn't his daughter screaming anymore, but himself.

Chapter 4

Aaliyah ran through the bedroom door to find her husband writhing on the floor, ripping out tufts of his hair and screaming. Katie knew better than to try and shake her father from his trance, so she turned on the lights in the room. Aaliyah fell to her husband's side, bit her wrist and shook her arm until the flow of blood covered it. The ceiling fan blew the scent of blood into her husband's nostrils and the scent wafted over him. Jayden's eyelids batted rapidly until his eyes were fully open and focused. Aaliyah reached her arm out cautiously toward Jayden. She let him drink from her open wound as she softly stroked his head with her other hand. She was so relieved that she couldn't scold him for not feeding before he went to sleep. He knew better and this was not the first time this had happened. In fact, the last time he had a nightmare like this, he slashed his own face to ribbons. Jayden is all too aware of the consequences and he is also aware that he will relive that dreaded night for the rest of his life. *Why on Earth would he do this to himself?* Aaliyah thought to herself. He's told her that he is looking for clues, but Aaliyah feels he's tormenting himself for not having saved his children. Aaliyah has begged him to stop tormenting himself this way. She knew deep down he blamed himself for what happened. He blamed himself that he couldn't save their children. He blamed himself that he was still alive and they were not. Aaliyah could hardly get out of bed some days, filled with pain, heart ache, and deep depression. Seeing her husband like this made her feel worse. She made a mental note to have another heart to heart with him. This can't keep happening. They still had one child who is also suffering, and they still had each other. For Aaliyah, that fateful night had been the worst of her life and she had a very different perspective of that evening.

* * *

Aaliyah was just stepping out of the restroom when a deafening roar sounded down the street causing the glass windows of the ice cream parlor to shake. In the distance she heard car alarms going off. Closing the restroom door, Aaliyah looked into the panic-stricken face of Katie.

"I heard a loud boom. I think it might have come from across the street where we parked the car. I called Dad and Brian and no one is answering. I'm scared mom."

Aaliyah opened the front door and peered down the street. She called to the young man working at the register.

"Call the police. Katie, let's go."

As the women walked down the street, they could hear the sounds of screaming in the distance.

"That's your father," Aaliyah said panicked. She had only heard him scream once before. It had been at a Jiu Jitsu tournament. His opponent had put him in a spine lock causing him to scream out before submitting. The women began running toward the parking garage. When the parking structure came into view they could see four people huddled around a person on the ground. As the smaller man reached toward the person on the ground, a loud screeching caused the group to look up. A black panel van roared toward the group with its high beams on. The group jumped back to avoid being hit. The van which had seemingly come out of nowhere came screeching to a halt next to the crumpled body on the floor. The burned rubber from the tires could be smelled from where Aaliyah and Katie stood across the street. The driver's door opened and a shadowy figure stepped out. Aaliyah could see the gathered strangers were taken aback by the lone beings sudden appearance. From beneath his long overcoat the newcomer pulled out two machine guns and began unleashing a barrage of bullets at the group. They all dove for cover as some of the rounds found their mark. Ripping holes through the assemblage as they dove for cover, the man discarded one of the guns and threw open the large panel door. With the dispersal of the coven, Aaliyah could now see the broken figure on the pavement was her husband. With uncanny speed, the maverick grabbed Jayden and tossed him in the van. He slammed the door shut, continuing to shoot as he climbed back into the driver's seat. With the engine still running, he shifted the van into drive and slammed on the gas, causing the tires to spin in place for a moment burning even more rubber. The van raced through the empty parking lot, blasted through a barrier and jumped a curb to reach the street. As the van bounced on to the street, sparks flew from the undercarriage. The van teetered, almost flipping over and quickly accelerated into the night. As it raced off, the group of people being shot at jumped into their SUV and peeled out, racing to catch up to the mysterious van. As they climbed into the vehicle, Aaliyah was horrified that the congregation who had just seemingly been shot to death were alive, let alone able to sprint into the waiting SUV to pursue her husband. When the coast was clear she and Katie stood up. Their ears were ringing from the gun fire but their fear of what had become of their family was their overarching thought.

They cautiously crossed the parking lot and approached the parking garage. Everything was drenched in blood. The rubble from the smashed valet attendant booth lay at the mouth of the entrance. They attempted to side step the shallow pools of blood that reflected the night in crimson. They headed into the parking garage, walking right past the still dying body of Brian. They didn't see him as his body had been discarded in landscaping shrubbery near the entrance. Aaliyah stood among the gore taking in the carnage. Her mind was numb. This surreal nightmare was passing over her in waves. It barely registered that Katie had slipped her hand into Aaliyah's, gripping it tightly. She could feel Katie trembling as they slowly ascended into the parking garage. It was then that Katie noticed as they passed a car her little sister's head sitting as a grotesque hood ornament on a red town car. Katie's shrill scream made Aaliyah jump. Aaliyah let go of Katie's hand and saw what her daughter saw. She stumbled back from the sight and nearly tripped over Jenny's decapitated corpse. Aaliyah's shocked mind tried to comprehend what had just transpired. Her daughter lay motionless on the ground and her husband was kidnapped. After what seemed like an eternity, she painfully knelt down at her little girl's body. Her whole being seemed to fill up with pain and agony with every inch she knelt closer. When she arrived at Jenny's little body, she slowly reached for the ripped up torso. Aaliyah pulled the limp body and held it close to her own. The abruptness of the night's events made it difficult for her to realize what was happening as she held her baby. She stared at Jenny's head a few feet away as she squeezed her eyes shut and screamed with all her might. "No, no, no," she yelled. She sobbed uncontrollably into the blood-soaked shirt of her little princess.

Katie had been frozen in place by the events that unfolded in front of her. She slowly backpedaled away from her mother. She was still transfixed on Jenny's head and couldn't seem to look away. Her gaze finally broke as she wondered what happened to her brother. She turned back toward the street and froze again abruptly. As she turned her head, she got her answer. She blinked several times as she approached his body. Brian was gently bleeding out of the holes in his torso and his chest was missing a chunk of flesh. He had almost no blood left in his body and his heart was about to give out. She ran to him, but at first was afraid to touch him. After several seconds, she kneeled down and reached for his face. Fighting for each breath, drowning in his own blood, he looked up at his sister. He tried to speak but could only cough up blood as he drifted away from his sister. Aaliyah appeared behind Katie and let out another guttural scream. She was just in time to see what life there was left in her son, slowly floating into oblivion.

* * *

Closing her bedroom door, Aaliyah glanced back at her husband who had returned to sleep after his nightmare. She shook her head, trying to clear her own memories and headed downstairs.

Chapter 5

Jayden didn't have the strength to keep from black-ing out in the back of the van. They drove for hours until the van finally came to a stop on a gravel road. Jayden could hear the driver's door open and close. He heard the gravel crunching with each step the driver took. The rear panel doors swung open and Jayden squinted at his kidnapper. Jayden felt himself being picked up and carried. His eyes were almost swollen shut. Ten teeth had been kicked out; his left leg and right hand were broken. His left hand and head had deep lacerations and he had a con-cussion. However, he could scarcely feel these inju-ries because the pain in his heart was so much more severe. He would later remember that the alternating pains were the only things that kept him conscious at that moment. Jayden could feel the cold wet dew on the grass as his captor laid him down. As he lay on the ground motionless, he heard a loud noise; it sounded like a big rock being dragged across con-crete. Jayden's mind was too fragmented to put any coherent thoughts together. "This is it, I'm ready to die," was the only logical thing that came to his mind. As he lay on the ground, he wondered why this man had taken him, when it appeared death was a foregone conclusion. Jayden was just reaching a state of full consciousness when he was lifted off the ground and brought into a dark room. *It is freezing,* he thought. He tried to lift his head and get a better look around, but couldn't. His kidnapper handled him the way Drake had, with ease. The man carrying him laid him down again, this time onto something that was hard, smooth and cold. Jayden rubbed his non-broken hand along the hard smooth marble he was laying on. As he squinted and forced his eyes to focus in the darkness of the room, he realized that the nightmare was continuing. The kidnapper was pulling a giant stone door into the entryway they had just come through. Jayden could see the silhouette of the man dragging the giant door and it wasn't Pagan or Drake.

"Who are you?" Jayden mumbled slowly. The words felt strange leaving his mouth because of the missing teeth.

"You need to rest; you just took a very severe beating," the man answered over his shoulder as he busied himself with something Jayden couldn't see.

Still not being able to lift his head, he closed his eyes for a moment. He could hear the man milling around the room, but he was doing it in the dark.

"What do you want?" Jayden asked cautiously into the darkness.

"You sure are talkative for someone that just went through what you went through," the man responded. "But if you must know, I simply want to live out my time here until I can be reunited with… my master." His kidnapper continued. "In a way, vampires are like all other beings in this universe; we yearn for what we cannot have." Jayden trained his eyes in the direction of the man's voice; he could barely make out a silhouette. He was considering the man's accent before the thought hit him, *Great, another freak who thinks he's a vampire!*

Jayden lay silent thinking of what Drake had said and what this person was telling him. He thought of how unbelievable what was happening was. *How could he seriously consider "Vampires" to be real? How could he believe his children were gone? How could he go on living? He lay motionless except for his head, which shook slowly from side to side.*

Jayden could still hear the man moving around the room, but he still couldn't see him. It was difficult for him to breathe, so he remained silent and tried to fight off the pain of his children and the uncertainty of his wife.

Tears began to roll down his cheeks.

"Please tell me this is a dream," he sobbed slowly into the darkness.

"I wish I could, but I cannot," the man answered as he lit a match and transferred the flame to a candle. Jayden turned his head quickly in the direction of the light,

"Who are you?" he asked as he stared at the dark figure.

"My name is Kristoff," the man answered slowly as he stared back at Jayden. Kristoff had a slight accent, Eastern European ... maybe Russian? Jayden tried to focus on the man's silhouette, from his swollen vision he noticed the man's movements were smooth and deliberate. His eyes were liquid like Drake's, except Kristoff had unbelievably blue eyes. The blue in Kristoff's eyes were the same as the waters of Saint Lucia, where Jayden and Aaliyah honeymooned. His straight shoulder length black and grey hair framed his thin face. His modern clothes, fit physique and good looks gave the impression of a youthful man. However, the sound of his voice and color of his hair made him seem more wise and seasoned,

Jayden's mouth was really bothering him now and he wanted to quit talking, but there were so many questions.

"What are you gonna do to me?" Jayden asked looking at Kristoff quizzically.

"For starters, I'm going to save your life. That is, if you want me to," Kristoff answered matter-of-factly. He turned his back and busied himself with something on a table behind him. Jayden searched for the right words to say, but his missing teeth and images of Brian and Jenny made it difficult to think and talk.

"You're not going to kill me?" Jayden asked slowly as he surveyed the room. Kristoff looked at Jayden over his shoulder, "I just said I was going to save your life, why would you ask if I was going to kill you?" Kristoff turned to face Jayden and crossed his arms across his chest. "That guy Drake was a vampire and you're a vampire," Jayden said trying to wrap his mind around all of this.

"Ah, Drake," Kristoff answered as he nodded his head up and down slowly, Jayden was looking harder at the walls.

"Hey, where are we?" Jayden asked. He tried to get up from the slab, but raising his head caused too much pain. "Is this a crypt or something?" Jayden asked cautiously.

"Yes, it's a mausoleum," Kristoff answered solemnly. "I am dying Kristoff. Please take me to a hospital."

"I don't think that would be in your best interest," Kristoff answered as he came closer to Jayden. Jayden began to weep as thoughts about his children came flooding back.

"Please tell me my kids aren't dead," he begged as he looked into Kristoff's eyes. "I can't tell you that either," Kristoff replied.

Looking into Kristoff's eyes reminded Jayden that real vampires were the issue here. Besides the pain the only thing that consumed his thoughts was his family. His mouth only had so many more words.

"Will you take me to my family?" he asked as he turned his head and looked away from Kristoff.

"I think you mean, what's left of your family don't you?" Kristoff asked. Jayden turned quickly to face Kristoff. Kristoff caught Jayden's stare and looked deep into his swollen eyes.

The comment had upset Jayden, but he remembered that vampires are real. He gave a menacing look at Kristoff, but dared not think about doing anything more. Kristoff half smiled as he stepped a little closer to Jayden.

He reached out and put his hand on Jayden's shoulder and said, "Your family is safe for now. Your wife and daughter will be surrounded by police for quite a while; Drake wouldn't dare go after them with so many people around. He gave chase for a brief while, but I managed to elude him. Besides, the sun should be coming up by the time the police are finished."

Jayden's mind was racing uncontrollably with incoherent fragmented thoughts and images. *How can I trust this person? Jenny being killed. Vampires cannot be real. Brian being eaten. My body hurts so bad. Everything is red. Those bullets damaged my hearing. Where is Katie? This slab is so cold. I'm going to die. I deserve to die. Where was God? There is no God. My head won't stop spinning. Aaliyah, Aaliyah, Aaliyah.*

His eyes rolling in his head, Jayden coughed blood all over his face.

Kristoff gently put his hand on Jayden's shoulder. "Please try to calm down Jayden. I'll try to answer all of your questions. Let's start with the easiest. Like I said before, my name is Kristoff and I am an immortal." Jayden gasped suddenly and stared at Kristoff; he had not gotten used to the mind reading thing.

"You said you were going to save my life, when are you going to get started?" Jayden asked in extreme pain. Kristoff moved back from Jayden and leaned against a large marble cross mounted on the wall. He paused a moment, rubbed his light beard and then looked seriously at Jayden.

"I didn't mean save your life in the traditional sense," he said. Jayden looked in confusion at Kristoff.

"What sense are you talking about then?"

"The sense that you will still be on earth, the sense that you will still be with your family and the sense that you will reach your destiny," Kristoff answered. Kristoff's answer worried Jayden. He didn't know why, but he became very nervous. Where he once feared for his life, he now feared for his soul. He felt as though he could start to see where this was going.

"Tell me how you're going to save me exactly," Jayden said.

"As I said earlier, only if you want me to," Kristoff informed him.

Several thoughts went through Jayden's mind, but the only one that made sense caused him to say, "I know I'm going to regret this, but are you talking about turning me into a vampire?" Kristoff stared at what was in his hands for what seemed like an eternity in silence before he answered.

"Turning is such a trite word, I prefer becoming," Kristoff finally said. Jayden's eyes hurt as they tried to widen. While he was suspecting that this would be the case, he did not expect Kristoff's answer. "You've lost too much blood to try and save you through conventional methods now. So, it's either my way or no way," Kristoff told him.

Is it better to die with Brian and Jenny? Should I just tell him to let me die? I mean how can I go on living without all my kids? Will this affect my immortal soul? No. I still have Katie and Aaliyah who need me. I can't give up. Kristoff rose up from the cross and began to walk around the room and stare at Jayden.

He watched Jayden as he shook his head violently "no". He watched as the signs of bleeding out were beginning to show. In five more minutes Jayden would be dead.

"What will happen if I take your offer? Is the movie stuff real?" Jayden asked nervously.

"Some is, some isn't," Kristoff answered as he continued to walk slowly around Jayden lying on the marble slab.

"Does it hurt? How long will it be before I can go back to my life? Can I go back to my life?" Jayden asked.

"I don't have all the answers, but I can tell you that you'll be dead shortly if you don't accept my offer soon," Kristoff answered as he stopped walking. "And if you accept my offer I will make you infinitely stronger. I will give you no more mortal worries. I will give you life and I will give it to you everlasting," Kristoff continued.

Jayden closed his eyes and pictured his daughter in the clutches of Drake and Brian being held up by Pagan. Without opening his eyes, he nodded his head in affirmation.

"I will explain everything in due time. Now lie back and know that the pain you endure will be over soon, but it will be replaced with a new kind of suffering." Kristoff said. He took the crucifix that he had been fashioning out of bone and placed it above Jayden's head on the marble slab.

Kristoff removed his jacket, pinned Jayden's arms to the marble slab and lowered his head until his mouth touched Jayden's neck. Kristoff sank his fangs into the tanned, soft flesh. Jayden felt the pain right away and screamed as Kristoff began to slowly drain him. The blood began to flow over Kristoff's eager tongue and ecstasy flowed through his brain. Jayden's body went stiff, his heart slowed down and his eyes rolled back into his head. Kristoff remained on Jayden's neck for only a moment, because of the massive amount of blood he had already lost. When Kristoff straightened his body, he continued to stare at Jayden; he was waiting for the after effects.

Within seconds Jayden could feel the fire coursing through his body. He jerked his head violently from side to side for a few seconds and then curled into the fetal position. He began to dry heave. A moment later the pain was so intense he could hardly breathe. Kristoff waited until death was a mere heartbeat away before he cut his wrist with his razor-sharp fingernail and placed the wound to Jayden's mouth. At first Jayden didn't drink Kristoff's blood. After waiting a moment more, Kristoff forced Jayden's mouth open and pushed his wrist into it.

Jayden still didn't suck Kristoff's wrist voluntarily, but the blood flowed into his mouth anyway. He held his breath for as long as he could, but his lung was pierced and he had to take a breath. He waited for the metallic taste and smell of blood to overwhelm him. To his surprise, Kristoff's blood tasted sweet, like honey. Jayden locked his lips onto Kristoff's wrist and sucked hard till the blood was rushing freely down his throat. As he drank, the pain intensified. His mind ran rampant with thoughts of his children. Through the blood he was able to personify his pain. Crystal images of his family growing up flooded him. The thumping of his heart was blasting in his ears. As he continued his feast for life, the beating grew fainter. And then, like an old clock he felt his heart stop beating. The pain was slowly subsiding. Amazingly, his lacerations were closing, and his broken hand began to curl around Kristoff's forearm. His shattered bones were fusing back together. He could feel the holes where his teeth had been knocked out being filled with new ones. In fact two of his new teeth were dagger sharp fangs. His skin was regenerating where it had been slashed away. The swelling in his eyes began to subside and he began to see clearly. Jayden swung his feet over the edge of the marble bed and sat up without letting go of Kristoff's arm. Kristoff tried to push Jayden's face away from his wrist, but Jayden had grown immensely stronger. He had formed a death grip on his new life source. Kristoff yelled for him to stop, but Jayden was consumed by the taste and effect of Kristoff's blood.

Kristoff placed his foot on Jayden's chest and pushed as hard as he could, falling to the ground in the process. He managed to break Jayden's grip and cursed as he pulled himself to his feet. He could see that the transformation was taking hold.

Once Kristoff broke Jayden's vise-like grip, Jayden stared at him hungrily with blood dripping from his chin as the metamorphosis began.

Acid coursed through Jayden's veins. The pain was wreaking havoc on his body, but his mind was playing tricks on him too. He kept seeing a collage of brutality. His son being killed. His daughter being killed. People being crucified and others decapitated. The visions were new and old. Present day and ancient. The culmination of all of this was driving him mad. All at once he could no longer stand the confines of the mausoleum. Too many new and strange sensations had overtaken him all at once and Jayden had reached the precipice of insanity. He pushed away from the marble slab and staggered toward the stone entrance of the mausoleum. Jayden easily shoved the stone door aside and erupted into the night.

As he stepped into the moonlight, it was like stepping into the midday sun. He shielded his eyes as they adjusted to the intense glare. As his eyes began to focus he noted that he was in an old cemetery in the middle of nowhere. He was able to gaze at the moon and see every crater in its face even though it was only a crescent this evening. Off to his left he could hear the thunderous sound of wings beating. When he looked, he saw a cicada was making the tremendous sound. As the tiny insect hovered, a bat swooped in like a hawk and devoured the bug. The event seemed to happen in slow motion. Ahead he saw crumbling grave stones. He could read the epitaphs all across the cemetery. Without warning, he began to run through the grave markers. Overgrown braches whipped him in the face as he sprinted.

Unconcerned with them, he picked up his speed. He crashed through the cement headstones and granite crosses like they were paper maché. Picking up speed, he careened through the cemetery spotting three intricately sculpted angel statues. The angels were posed in reverence, giving glory to God. He darted at the first one and punched the head clean off. He grabbed the wings on the next one and ripped them off. Then he kicked it, obliterating it all together. Grabbing the last one, he hurled it into the night. It soared well over a hundred yards before crashing resoundingly to the earth like a meteor. Turning around he saw a massive granite cross well over twelve feet tall. It stood adjacent to where the angels had been. He exploded toward it at full speed. Spearing the cross, it cracked at the base. Jayden then mounted the grounded cross, pounding the granite into dust. He roared at the top of his lungs, cursing God. Each punch caused a deeper crater in the earth. The intense rush of the blood was beginning to subside. He was suddenly feeling weaker. He stood up and began walking toward the end of the cemetery. He walked very slowly and deliberately as the hate in his heart was crushing him now. It was then that he happened upon a very unique statue. The sight of it stopped him in his tracks. It was a stone angel kneeling beside a child's coffin. The weeping angel's wings were spread over the coffin as the angel mourned the child inside. Jayden fell to his knees. This sculpture reflected his own sorrow. It was then that he thought of Aaliyah and the pain she must be in. She would have to deal with this pain on her own if Jayden didn't return to her.

How can I go back? What do I say to her? She will not believe any of this.

Holding his face in his hands and crying, Jayden's body was racked with uncontrollable sobs. His tears were no longer water, but blood. The blood tears flowed through his fingers and down his arms. Then, out of nowhere he felt a strong hand on his back. It was Kristoff. Kristoff allowed him to weep for a few more moments in silence. He then helped Jayden to his feet.

"You must feed soon. You exerted a great deal of energy and you are only a fledgling vampire. You will need to eat more often than I do," Kristoff said.

Jayden nodded his head, although he didn't fully understand what Kristoff was saying. He wiped his face with his forearm only to see that it was covered in blood. He took off his tattered shirt and started wiping himself clean. As he was wiping himself off, he paused as he noticed something was very different.

Where once his stomach was soft and large, it was now rock hard and flat. He ran his fingers over his newly formed six-pack. His shoulders had striations where previously there had been none. His veins were popping out through the thin skin of his now overdeveloped biceps. Jayden looked up at Kristoff who was observing the changes as well.

"What the hell?" Jayden asked.

"What the hell indeed," Kristoff responded as he smiled at Jayden. "I have only created one other vampire before you, so my ancient blood should make you quite powerful." Jayden flexed his new muscles. Even at the peak of his physical prowess he hadn't been this ripped.

"A life saved," Kristoff said smugly.

"What now?" Jayden asked as he dropped the bloody shirt.

"How would you like an opportunity to avenge your family?" Kristoff asked.

"How?" Jayden asked, surprised. He knew how strong Drake was. He also knew what his coven could do. "How could I ever be strong enough to beat him at anything?" Jayden asked.

"With my help." Kristoff responded.

"I will do whatever it takes to kill them all," Jayden replied angrily. "I will bring this war against Drake and anyone else who is responsible…even God."

Kristoff placed the small bone cross into Jayden's hand.

"Try to understand my young fledgling; while your quest for revenge extends to the heavens it is not God who wanted this for you." Jayden closed his hand around the small object and squeezed. When his hand reopened, there was nothing but dust.

"God did nothing to save my family. For his sake he better hope the atheists are right and he doesn't exist."

Chapter 6

Jayden started for the van, but Kristoff stopped him. "What?" Jayden asked. Kristoff grabbed the bridge of his nose with his thumb and index finger.

"We aren't taking the van," Kristoff replied, slightly annoyed.

"How are we going to get wherever we're going then?" Jayden asked.

"It's a good night for a little jog," Kristoff suggested. Jayden looked Kristoff up and down and then said jokingly, "You don't look dressed to jog."

"We'll see. Do you know where City Hall is?" Kristoff asked.

Jayden looked at the street signs in the distance. They were miles outside of Boulder City. They were at least ten miles away from the city limits and nowhere close to Las Vegas.

"I don't think running is the best idea," Jayden said. Kristoff stared at Jayden a moment and then grabbed his hand.

"Let's go," Kristoff said as he began pulling Jayden. Jayden grudgingly let himself be led. Kristoff started out jogging for a few feet, but within a few seconds they were running faster than the traffic on the 95 freeway. Kristoff soon let go of Jayden's hand and Jayden was surprised to see that he could run fast on his own. He was moving even faster than he had in the cemetery. They had reached the highway in less than three seconds and were now running alongside it. Jayden could barely believe what was happening.

"How do you like it?" Kristoff asked above the sound of the wind. Jayden was achieving amazing speeds with minimal effort.

The wind was rushing past Jayden's face as he squinted into it.

"I could get used to this," Jayden replied. He wasn't getting tired, and the city was blurring past him. He put his head down and decided to give a little more effort. Less than a minute later he slowed enough to see the street signs; he had overshot City Hall by ten blocks. He slowed to a stop and turned around. When he got back to the front of City Hall, Kristoff was waiting and chuckling.

"Where were you going?" Kristoff asked. Jayden smirked and brushed off the ribbing. It was one o'clock in the morning, but the night was illuminated as if it were one o'clock in the afternoon.

"I can see better at night than I ever did in the day," Jayden remarked. He closed his eyes and breathed in deeply. He could smell the grass that had been cut earlier that night. He could smell the asphalt of the street. He could even smell the cleaning solution the janitors used inside the City Hall building.

"Let's go across the street to the park," Kristoff suggested.

Jayden opened his eyes and followed suit. Jayden was pleased with how nice the new park was since its renovation. When he was growing up, graffiti covered the playground equipment like hieroglyphics and homeless people encircled the park like a human border. Now the park had desert landscape where the homeless used to sleep and all the playground equipment was new.

"Now, I need you to focus," Kristoff told him.

"On what?" Jayden inquired with a perplexed look.

Kristoff ran his hand through his hair impatiently.

"I have only created two Vampires in my entire time on this planet. Partly because I'm impatient, so please try to keep up. Strength is only one component of your new life," Kristoff said.

Strength is the only thing I'm thinking about, Jayden thought.

"You're going to need more than strength if you intend on beating Drake," Kristoff told him. Again, Jayden looked at Kristoff in amazement, because again Kristoff had read his mind.

"So what else do I need?" Jayden asked.

"There is so much to learn; most of your education will come from experience. But I can let you know a few attributes, at least enough to keep you alive and make your life better," Kristoff began. "For instance, in case you haven't noticed, you can descend and retract your fangs. You can also descend them further for fighting, or to warn others to stay away. It is called raging. This requires a little emotional control. It will happen naturally if you are angry or fearful." Kristoff demonstrated by closing his eyes and opening his mouth wide. When his eyes opened, his face had distorted. His cheek bones and brow line were more pronounced. His eyes had sunk deeper within his skull and seemed to crystallize. His fangs had descended nearly to his bottom lip. His ferocious appearance was both fearsome and terrifying. His good looks had dissolved from his face and all that remained was ugliness and pure hatred. After waiting for Jayden to take this all in, he closed his eyes again and his face returned to its original state of serenity.

Jayden tried extending his fangs twice and felt he had it under control after that. While he couldn't yet rage, Kristoff assured him he would do it out of instinct when he needed to. While pleased with his new powers, he secretly feared unleashing this new found ability. Even before his family was slain, he knew that his emotions were a tempest. He could easily hurt an innocent person without control of this power. He had been docked more than a few points for losing his patience in a match and slamming his opponent. He would need more than a couple of hours to learn how to handle his new found powers.

"What else can I do?" Jayden asked emphatically.

Kristoff nodded for Jayden to follow him. It took Jayden a second to realize that Kristoff was about to start running again. When he did he had to push himself to catch up to his new master. Las Vegas City Hall is located on Las Vegas Boulevard and Stewart, they headed south on Las Vegas Boulevard to the resort that resembled the city of New York, located at the corner of Tropicana, six miles away. Although the glitzy veneer had faded for Jayden, there was no denying that the Las Vegas strip was one of the most amazing places in the world. The lights on the strip made the street look like its own galaxy. The cars and people lit up the night with so much energy that Jayden had to close his eyes and cover his ears, while he tried to control his new hyper senses. Opening his eyes back up he was now very aware of where he was. He looked down the street towards a night club that he used to be a bouncer at when he was younger. It reminded him of the unique position that people growing up in this town were put in.

The famous people that frequented Vegas were so common that even B-list celebrities were turned away from night clubs. This was a town built on crime, perfected by ambition, and thrived on dreams. This was the real "City That Never Sleeps". The casinos' tricks ensured that you lived in their world and not your own. There weren't any windows to let you know if it was night or day. There were no clocks on the walls to let you know you had been gambling for more than twenty-four hours. The alcohol was free and flowed like the Nile twenty-four hours a day. Jayden had read that vampires often choose places like New Orleans and Paris to live, but he thought, *If you could only live at night for the rest of your life, what better place in the world is there to spend eternity than Las Vegas?*

Tourists were looking at Jayden as they walked by, partly because he was shirtless and also because of the blood that still stained his torso. Jayden suddenly became very aware that he was being gawked at. Kristoff read his mind and with lightning speed stepped into a tourist shop. Pulling a shirt from the rack he bolted back outside to a waiting Jayden. He had gone and returned in under a second. Jayden pulled the novelty shirt over his head.

"How is it that no one can see us when we run?"

"We move too quickly. They can't see us until after we have come to a stop," Kristoff answered.

"Oh," Jayden said as he looked around at the tourists milling about as if it were broad daylight. It was 1:30 in the morning. Kristoff looked Jayden up and down and surveyed his tattered clothes.

"I think we should get you some more suitable clothes. Come on," Kristoff said, turning for the entrance of the resort, where the retailers and men's clothing stores never closed. Jayden looked down at his clothes; his shirt was two sizes too small. His pants, socks, and shoes were ragged and covered in blood. His fingernails had dried blood under them and his forearms were powdered in granite from the statues he destroyed. He shrugged and took off after Kristoff.

The sales woman looked disdainfully at Jayden as the two men walked into the high class Italian men's store. "Can I help you?" she locked eyes with Kristoff.

"You're going to dress my friend," Kristoff told her. The woman's demeanor changed as she turned to face Jayden. "I'm going to dress you, sir," she murmured.

"You're going to give him the finest suit you have. He will also require a pair of shoes, along with anything else he needs," Kristoff said.

"I bet you would look good in Tom Bell or Versace. Come with me, sir," she said as she continued to stare at Jayden. Jayden looked at Kristoff, who raised his eyebrows and gestured for him to follow the woman. The sales woman did not leave Jayden, even though several customers entered the store while he was there. She even went as far as to get water for Jayden to clean up. After Jayden had cleaned up and was looking sharp, he walked out of the dressing room to find Kristoff talking to the sales woman near the cash register. There were ten people in the store, but the woman still didn't take her eyes off of Kristoff. The woman handed Jayden a bag with old clothes in it and handed her card to Kristoff "Call me."

"You paid her, right?" Jayden asked as they walked out of the store.

"Sort of," Kristoff smirked nonchalantly as he continued to walk.

Jayden paused. "What did you do to her?"

"A very good question, one that brings me to your next lesson," Kristoff responded, looking around the casino. He noticed a 5'10", curvy, raven-haired server. The beauty was serving drinks at a high rollers' Blackjack table. Kristoff pointed at her. "Do you see her? I want you to go over. Look into her eyes and talk to her," Kristoff instructed.

"What should I say?" Jayden mumbled.

"Oh, I'm sure you'll think of something," Kristoff answered

Rebecca was her name and getting attention was her game. At 5'10," 140 pounds, striking green eyes and black hair, the Egyptian goddess had a smile that made you blush. She was dressed in her normal attire for work; a well-fitting one-piece leotard, four-inch heels, and nothing else. She didn't object to wearing the skimpy outfit; she loved the attention and she earned more money because of it. Her family asked more of her professionally -they wanted her to put her Bachelors of Science in Biology to use— but she ignored them because she earned more money a year than both of her college-educated parents combined.

After serving the wealthy gamers, Jayden saw her stop and pick up a glass from a slot machine, admiring herself in the reflective metal. Her intuition told her that someone was standing close behind. *This pervert behind me is staring at my ass,* she thought. She whipped around. "Can I help you, si–?" She made eye contact with Jayden just as she was finishing her question.

Jayden sensed something was different. He just didn't know what. "Can I get a drink please?"

Rebecca was flustered. This never happened to her. She sputtered out a response.

"Sure. What can I get you?"

Jayden could feel the growing connection between them. He could feel the woman's heartbeat in his veins. He reached out and touched her cheek with the back of his hand. She drew in a deep breath of excitement as he let his hand drift down her neck and over her breasts. He let his hand linger for a moment before withdrawing it. Knowing that the casinos never served top shelf liquor to the general public he made a request she should have denied.

"Would you mind getting me a bottle of your finest cognac?"

Rebecca smiled coyly.

"Of course…Is there anything else I can do for you?"

Jayden shook his head. Rebecca smiled and turned towards the bar while Jayden walked back over to Kristoff.

"Do you know what power you just exerted?" Kristoff asked.

"Yeah, I have freaking Jedi mind control." Both men began to laugh. Kristoff nodded with his head for Jayden to turn around. As Jayden turned around, he saw Rebecca walking quickly towards him. She did not take her eyes off of Jayden as she approached.

"There you are. I thought you'd left. Here's your drink," she said as she extended the glass in her hand. "It's Remy Martin Black Pearl Louis XIII. It costs $55,000 a bottle or $1,500 per drink," she added. Jayden took the glass and looked quizzically at Kristoff. Knowing he hadn't paid her anything he pushed a little further.

"What about my change? Don't you still owe me about five hundred dollars?"

Rebecca reached into her pocket and produced a wad of cash, counting it out.

"Here's three hundred, four hundred and five hundred." She offered the money to Jayden. He looked at the smiling Kristoff, looked back at Rebecca and then took the cash from the beautiful woman. "Are you going to stay?" she asked.

Jayden didn't know what to make of this woman; she never took her eyes off of him. "No, I've got to go. You go back inside and go back to work," he instructed. She walked backwards away from him. Jayden gestured for her to run along. She was thirty feet away when she finally decided to turn around. "Well, I'll be damned," Jayden said in amazement.

"You sure are," Kristoff responded as he turned to head for the exit. Jayden tilted the glass up, shoved the cash in his pocket, threw his old clothes in the trash and walked quickly to catch up. As he set the empty glass down he gave pause.

"I thought vampires could only drink blood? I mean won't the alcohol make me sick or something," Jayden asked?

"The blood sustains us. It is our life force. But we can in fact have alcohol. We feel the effects less than mortals, but if we combined the alcohol with blood, we become very intoxicated," Kristoff said.

As they walked outside, a rollercoaster raced overhead. "Come with me," Kristoff instructed. They walked to the point of the track that was closest to the ground. Kristoff waited for the rail car to return. When he saw it approaching he opened his mouth and shouted his name. The people out on the street looked around, they thought a fighter jet was flying low overhead. Jayden clamped his hands over his ears. The sound was deafening—even the people on the rail car ducked. "What the hell was that?"

"It's another bonus of Becoming," Kristoff answered, pointing to his diaphragm. "You scream from here. The sound will be amplified ten thousand times." Kristoff paused, lost in thought.

"What?"

"I want to show you one more thing, but it's getting late." Kristoff pointed to his watch, and tapped on 3:00am. He turned and started striding toward the rear of the hotel. "Come on." Upon arriving, Kristoff looked at his surroundings to make sure no one was around. He held his arms outstretched by his side. "Watch closely," he instructed. Jayden's eyes widened as he saw Kristoff's feet leaving the ground.

"Oh, shit."

Kristoff smoothly levitated skyward to the third floor as Jayden looked on in amazement. He hung, suspended in midair for a second, and then sent his body into a spin like an ice skater. He spun and spun, then lowered himself back down to the ground. "I can do that?" Jayden asked excitedly.

"You have the basics, but you will have to practice to be that good. Now you try," Kristoff said.

"Do I have to hold my arms out?" Jayden poised himself.

"You don't have to, but it helps with your stability." Jayden held his arms out. "Now what?"

"Think 'up'. Or 'rise'," Kristoff answered. Jayden slammed his eyes shut and did as Kristoff told him. *Up.* He did as he was told. He briefly floated inches above the ground before falling back to earth.

"Don't worry about it," Kristoff said. "It takes time and practice to be able to ascend. You may try again later. For now we must go," Kristoff consoled.

"Where are we going?" Jayden asked.

"It's going to be light in a couple of hours. We have to find a place to sleep."

"What about the crypt?" Jayden asked.

"That's more of a safe house, "Kristoff answered as he turned the corner and headed back for the front of the hotel.

"Well, I've got $500 if we need money." Jayden hustled to keep up with his mentor.

"We don't need it," Kristoff said, reaching the registration desk. The receptionist looked up at the well-dressed ageless man as Kristoff approached. "Hello," she said.

Kristoff met her gaze. "Hello. You're going to give me your penthouse suite for two nights and I don't want to be disturbed."

"Yes, sir," the woman said as she scurried to secure the room. "What's your name, sir?"

"Kristoff, and no more questions," Kristoff shot back.

"Yes sir," the woman said apologetically. Jayden was in awe of his mentor. The woman gave Kristoff the room number and key. "Thank you," she said. Kristoff took it without a word, then turned and headed for the elevators with Jayden following close behind.

"Sunrise is coming," Kristoff said with a straight face as they entered the elevator. He pushed the "PH" button and then continued, "You're young and still have a lot of melanin in your skin. The older you get, the more sensitive you will become to the sun. Vampirism is not all gifts; it comes with curses. It eats away the melanin in your skin until you become like me. I can't bear more than a few seconds in the sun before I start to burn."

"Will you burst into flames?" Jayden joked.

Kristoff glared at Jayden. "No, it's slow and agonizing. Think of the worst sunburn you ever got. Now imagine it continuing until your skin melts off."

Jayden stared at Kristoff in silence. "Also, our existence must remain a secret. This isn't a television series. If you let our secrets be known, we will be hunted and humans have the weapons and technology to destroy us."

The elevator dinged as they reached the penthouse floor. Kristoff slid the electronic key card into the slot and pushed the door when it turned green. They entered the room. It was bigger than Jayden's house. He walked into one of the bedrooms to see a modern décor laid out in front of him.

"Two thousand square feet and only one bed? Guess I'll sleep on the couch," he said.

"There are two bedrooms," Kristoff replied as he removed his coat and headed for the blackout drapes. "Ok then, can I call my wife?"

"If you must," Kristoff replied. Jayden hurried for the phone. "Wait. Before you call, I must insist that you don't tell her what's happened to you yet. You will have a decision to make as to whether or not you want to involve your family. Tell your wife that she's not safe at home. I have to go out for a while," Kristoff said as he picked up his jacket and headed for the door. "Where are you going?" Jayden asked.

"I'm stepping out for a moment, you drained me pretty good. I have to eat now. I'll be back in a couple of hours," Kristoff said as the door clicked shut.

"OK," Jayden said as he picked up the phone. Jayden pondered what to say to Aaliyah. *Hi, how are you? Our son and daughter were murdered tonight and I'm staying in a penthouse?* He sighed and started dialing. The phone rang four times before Aaliyah's voice mail picked up. " … *To leave a message after the tone, press one.*"

"Aaliyah, it's me. I'm safe. I love you. Take Katie and go to your father's house. Our house isn't safe anymore. I'll see you tomorrow."

* * *

It was 6 a.m. and the sun was coming up. Aaliyah and Katie sat side by side outside the morgue on hard, blue, plastic chairs and watched television. The ambulance ride from the parking structure was pointless; it only served to get them away from the police questionings and media frenzy. The news reporter's voice on the television rang in her ears.

"The brutal murder of two Valley children and the kidnapping of their father leave a family confused and destroyed."

Katie leaned in and whispered to her mother, "Do you think Daddy's okay?"

Aaliyah buried her face in Katie's shoulder so that she couldn't see the lie in her eyes. "I'm sure he's going to be fine honey," Aaliyah said sobbing into Katie's shoulder. After a minute of soaking Katie's shirt with tears she continued, "We'll go home and get cleaned up. Then after some rest, we'll go back to the police station."

Aaliyah glanced down at her cell phone. *No Signal.* She turned her cell phone off to save the battery which hadn't been charged since before they left for the football game.

Chapter 7

It was 8:00 a.m. when Ronin Waddilove's eyes fluttered as the morning sun blasted into his living room. Beer bottles lay strewn about the room; payment from Jayden for calling the play that stopped Elko, a sign that his wife was no longer living there. Ronin stood up and stumbled to his son's closed bedroom door. Ronin was dressed in boxer shorts and a wife beater. He kicked at dirty clothes on the floor as he stumbled. Ronin was about to open James' door when he noticed the do-not-disturb sign hanging on the knob. The sign indicated that his son had company and that he shouldn't knock. The father and son now had more of a roommate living arrangement than a father/son relationship. It didn't bother Ronin at all, because he was all but out of the dating scene, thus he didn't have a big need for privacy. Ronin reached the kitchen and opened the refrigerator door; he grabbed for two things, a slice of pizza and a beer. *Nothing like cold pizza and beer first thing on a Saturday morning,* he thought as he bit into a slice of pepperoni, getting mentally prepared for a full slate of college football on TV. He scratched himself, thwacked the power button on the remote and the picture on his projector TV (his greatest pride and joy next to his boy and his truck) slowly appeared. His eyes were still on the TV as the can was still tilted on his lips and Aaliyah's puffy, tear-stained face was on the screen. He quickly took the can from his mouth, turned up the volume and watched intently. Aaliyah was crying and Katie stood behind her rubbing her back.

"Please, if you have any information, please call the police."

The news anchor appeared. "So far, the only information we have is that two children were brutally slain and their father was kidnapped from the Slavin parking garage on Paradise Road. We've received reports that massive amounts of blood were found at the scene and their bodies had been mutilated. We'll keep you updated as more information is received on this horrific tragedy–now dubbed the 'Sin City Massacre". This is Jared Newsome, Action News. Back to you Jessy…"

Ronin waited a second before slamming his beer down and dropping the slice of pizza onto the coffee table in front of him. He then ran to James' bedroom and beat on the door.

"Yeah." He heard the sound of clothes rustling.

"It's me, get up," Ronin yelled.

"What's up, pop?" James asked as he opened up the door, bleary-eyed. Ronin looked past his son and in to the room, seeing the mess and the young woman adjusting her spaghetti straps.

"Call Katie. Lose the chick," Ronin said as he turned to leave.

James looked confused. "Come on, Dad. It's hella early and don't call her that. Her name is Jaime." Ronin stopped and looked back at him.

The young woman snapped while staring at both men. "Actually, it's Janey. And don't worry; I drove last night in case you were too drunk to remember."

Ronin dismissed the young woman's snark and continued on to his bedroom. He rummaged through a pile of clothes on a chair and settled on a pair of gym shorts, tee shirt and flip flops. He heard James walk Janey to the front door. "I'll call you later," James said. Ronin grabbed his keys, cell phone and wallet. "Did you call Katie?" he called to James.

"Not yet."

"Get dressed and call Katie. Now. I'll be in the truck and hurry up," Ronin snapped.

"Where are we going?"

"Just do what I told you and hurry up!"

"Dad, what the hell is going on?" James asked as he closed the truck door.

"Have you called Katie?" Ronin asked again, ignoring James's question.

"Not yet," James replied as he reached for his cell phone.

"Call her now, like I told you to and find out where she is." Ronin threw the truck in reverse.

By the time Ronin put the truck into Drive, he heard James say "The morgue? Dad, they're at Clark County Morgue."

"We're on our way," James said before the call was unexpectedly cut off.

James looked at the phone and then his father. "What the hell's going on Dad?" he asked. "I don't know exactly, but I think at least one of the Endsleys is dead."

Chapter 8

Jayden woke up at 6:00 p.m., in the New York-style resort. He stretched, surprised that his new body was still around. He inspected his physique for a few minutes before he got out of bed. When he did get up, Kristoff was already awake, brewing coffee and reading the newspaper at the dinette table. "How did you sleep?" Kristoff asked.

"Not bad," Jayden shrugged, sinking into a couch a few feet from Kristoff. "I felt like I should be sleeping in a coffin."

"Some of our kind does sleep in coffins and others have different means of obtaining rest, but I find those methods a tad bit archaic," Kristoff shot back, never taking his eyes off of the newspaper.

"Wait, you drink coffee too?" Jayden observed.

"No, I don't. I just enjoy the smell actually," Kristoff remarked.

Jayden hopped to his feet. "So what's the next move?"

"First and foremost, you're going to take a shower. Then we'll get our night started. I took the liberty of buying you some new clothes. They're over there." He pointed to a pile of bags in a chair in the corner of the suite.

Minutes later, Jayden turned on the water and climbed into the oversized shower. He was taken aback when the water began to rain down from the ceiling upon him. He began to run his finger over a scar on his eyebrow, surprised that it didn't heal during the transformation. He remembered the day he got the scar. It was a hot, sunny Las Vegas day and he had taken the kids to the only water park in Las Vegas; Wet & Wild. The kids were excited, but it had been a bad day for Jayden. For starters, Jenny had brought a SpongeBob bed sheet instead of a towel, so now she'd have to use his and he would have to drip dry. Next, the car had gotten a flat tire on the way to the water park. Then his credit card was declined at the ticket booth. Jayden went to a nearby ATM, got cash and then he got back in line to purchase the tickets. Katie refused to put on her bathing suit; she wanted to wear cutoff jeans and a tee shirt instead. Finally, the kicker of the day, a gust of wind had picked up Jenny's rubber raft and as he was chasing it down he slipped on the wet concrete and cut his eyebrow open. He needed ten stitches to close the cut. The morning following the Wet & Wild fiasco, he woke up sore and tired, but, his ills seemed to subside when he opened his eyes to see a tray with breakfast sitting on the nightstand next to his bed with a thank you card from his wife and children. No one came into the room as he ate. He ate in silence, wondering where everyone was. He headed for the kitchen to put his dishes in the sink after his meal and found a note from Aaliyah saying they'd be back in a couple of hours and to enjoy his rest. He was surprised to see the kids had cleaned the house. He put his dishes in the sink and grabbed the card from the tray and opened it. Inside it simply said "Thank you, Dad." All the kids signed it and Jenny had drawn a sun on the inside of it.

Jayden continued to stroke the old scar, grateful that it hadn't healed. Jayden slightly opened the sliding glass door and yelled out to Kristoff, "That trick I used on the cocktail waitress and had her falling all over herself…how does that work?"

"It's kind of complicated," Kristoff shouted back.

Jayden turned the water off and walked to the doorway of the bedroom. "Can you simplify it for me?" Jayden asked.

Kristoff tossed the newspaper on the table. "There are three components to it; sight, smell and telepathy. It's not really that difficult in the grand scheme of things. Humans can do it also; they just haven't learned how to use their brains to the fullest capacity."

"What about the other two?" Jayden asked as he dried off in the doorway.

"The second is sight, unless the person is blind in which case you have the other two to fall back on. You enter the telepathic route to the brain through the eyes. If only humans knew the truth about the eyes being the window to the soul, it would eliminate a lot of needless turmoil for them.

"And the last is smell, pheromones to be specific. We have the ability to exhort them whenever we want to. Animals do it all the time, whenever it's time to mate. The difference is that our pheromones have intoxicating properties," Kristoff yelled out as Jayden got dressed in the next room.

"Does it work on *everyone?*" Jayden yelled back.

"It hasn't failed me in two thousand years," Kristoff answered.

"Will it work on other vampires?"

"No, and it won't work on Drake, so stop thinking that," Kristoff said as he stood up from the table and opened the drapes, gazing down across the City of Lights. "It works on humans and some animals. Actually, it's the reason why some people think we can turn into animals. We can get animals to do our bidding. That is a much harder skill to master, though."

"That's pretty incredible," Jayden said as he stepped from the bedroom wearing an off white, three piece Bernini suit and beige loafers. "But it's a little ostentatious, don't you think?" Jayden asked as he strutted proudly to Kristoff's side and looked out into the city.

Kristoff looked Jayden up and down.

"Are you talking about the pheromones or that suit?"

"Don't hate. I haven't worn a suit like this in years. Besides, I don't understand why we have to look like the cover of a GQ magazine," Jayden shot back. Kristoff had changed into a black suit with red pinstripes and black shoes. His hair was thick, slick and flowed behind him like a lion's mane.

"I choose to style myself in the times that I live in. Forgive me if I would rather not dress as a peasant," Kristoff stated.

Jayden rolled his eyes.

"Enough joking around, Jayden. We must now find your family and get the book," Kristoff said.

Jayden grabbed Kristoff by the arm as he tried to walk out the door.

"Stop," Jayden said. "I will help you do whatever is necessary to kill Drake, but there is something I must do first and I need your help."

Chapter 9

Jayden and Kristoff strutted into the morgue at 7:00 p.m. It was after hours and no one was at the front desk when the two men entered. They proceeded into the "waiting room", a refrigerated room where bodies are kept until they are autopsied and/or embalmed. A female coroner's assistant was standing on the other side of the door when they entered. "I'm sorry gentlemen, you can't come back here."

Jayden looked into her eyes and said, "We are going to look for two bodies and you're going to go and get some coffee."

"If you gentlemen will excuse me, I'm going to get some coffee," she said as she pushed through the double doors and left the room. "Not bad," Kristoff said, nodding his head in approval. Jayden didn't say anything as he turned and looked at the twelve bodies with toe tags, covered with white sheets. The two men began checking toe tags. Kristoff found Brian first and Jayden found Jenny moments later, pulling the sheet back and seeing his baby girl. Her head had not yet been reattached; it was set loosely on the torso. His eyes began to fill with crimson tears. He touched her cold face and then buried his face in her chest. He heaved with sobs, tried to straighten his body and stared at her face just a few seconds longer. He then covered her back up.

Brian's head had several bite marks on it and his throat was gone. Thankfully, the coroner had washed away some of the blood. Jayden gripped his son's shoulders tightly and began to cry again.

Kristoff left the room, allowing Jayden his time to mourn. Minutes later, Jayden emerged through the double doors with his son's body wrapped up in the sheet and over his shoulder. "Get Jenny," he instructed Kristoff.

Kristoff moved without a word and placed Jenny's body over his shoulder and her head under his left arm. Jayden opened the double doors leading outside and surveyed the area. Once he was sure no one was present, he pushed the door all the way open and began to run into the night. Kristoff ran through the door before it could close with Jenny's head firmly under his arm.

It only took them four minutes to reach Red Rock Canyon, a remote mountainous area ten miles outside of Vegas. They built makeshift pyres and laid the bodies on top of them. Kristoff remained silent as Jayden kissed his children for the last time.

"I'm going to get the people who did this, I promise you both. I gave my soul to do so and I won't rest until those motherfuckers are dead." Jayden cried. Kristoff watched and listened as Jayden cried and his volume increased. "I'll declare war on the whole world and heaven itself to get them, kids. Daddy promises," Jayden whispered through a clenched jaw.

Kristoff helped Jayden to his feet and told him to stand back. Kristoff then lit the shrubbery they were using as kindling under the bodies. The two men watched as the fire burned brightly in the canyon. Once the fire had burned down, Jayden turned to Kristoff. "I've got one last thing I have to do and then we can go."

The men ran to Palm Mortuary and Jayden knelt down in the rose garden beside the lake. A small wall with the names of those who had died ran parallel to the water. Jayden found the name of his grandparents and traced his hands over the letters. He then etched the names of his children in the same style lettering beneath his grandparents' names using his razor-sharp fingernails.

Chapter 10

It was 8:30 p.m. and inside of the Endsley residence, Ronin sat two feet away from Aaliyah. Aaliyah's hands were shaking and she sobbed as she retold the tale. Ronin reached out and held her hand. He thought it sounded a little crazy. He didn't say so. James sat across the room and listened intently. Katie reentered the room from the kitchen carrying two sodas, a wine cooler and a beer. Katie handed out the refreshments and then sat down next to James.

"I- I haven't even heard from Jayden. The police don't have any leads," Aaliyah concluded.

James opened his soda and leaned back. *I'm gonna need something stronger than this.* He looked at Katie fidgeting with her hair and tears welling in her eyes. *Poor girl, she needs to get out of this house.*

"Hey, Dad, if it's cool with Mrs. Endsley, can I take Katie for a drive to get some fresh air?"

"Her mother doesn't need to be alone tonight ..." Ronin started to say.

Aaliyah cut him off. "Actually, I think it's a good idea. Let her clear her head."

James stood up and offered his hand to Katie. He put his arm around her as they headed for the door.

Outside of the Endsley home was different. James and Katie had to dodge the police force foot traffic they encountered on their way to his car in the driveway. The Metropolitan Police Department had assigned 6 people to the case; two hostage negotiators and four homicide detectives.

Katie hardly noticed the traffic, as she was still in shock from what she had witnessed in the parking garage. Despite the crush she'd had on James since she was twelve, she didn't even notice his arm around her as they approached the car.

Ronin stood and looked out of the window and watched James back out of the driveway as the two negotiators approach the door. The doorbell rang. Ronin told Aaliyah to stay seated as he headed for the door. He stopped short of the door. "Any idea of what happened to Jay?" Ronin asked.

"None," she answered, hanging her head.

"It looks like the police are here to do their thing," Ronin said as the doorbell rang a second time.

"Are you going to go out and look for him?"

"I don't know if I should. I might be better off staying here," Ronin answered.

"I would feel better if you did go out and ask some questions and look around. Knowing that something is being done makes me feel more confident that we'll find him," She said in a sad, but assured tone. The doorbell rang a third time and Ronin opened the door. "Good evening. Is Mrs. Endsley here?"

"Come in." Ronin escorted the two men into the house.

"Good evening ma'am. I'm Sergeant Duncan and this is Sergeant McCoy of the Las Vegas Hostage Negotiation Squad." He continued talking with

Aaliyah about Jayden's disappearance. After five minutes, Ronin started getting restless and excused himself, telling Aaliyah that he was going to leave. She walked Ronin to the door. On their way to the door, Ronin instructed her to make sure that her phone was on. "I'll call you if I come up with anything." Ronin surveyed the area outside of Aaliyah's house before walking slowly out the door.

She closed the door and turned around, bumping into the negotiators. "We're going to be leaving now, ma'am."

"What?" Aaliyah asked, surprised that they were leaving.

"Well, there hasn't been any contact from the kidnappers and we don't have any leads."

"Aren't you going to tap my phone or something?" she asked, seeming confused.

"That's only in the movies ma'am. We don't have the resources right now. It's been twenty-four hours and there hasn't been a request for ransom or anything. Right now, we're hoping he's alive," McCoy informed her. "So, I can only sit here helpless and hope? You guys aren't going to do anything else to find my husband? Go, just get out and go," Aaliyah agitatedly insisted, her voice starting to shake. She ushered the two men to the door without saying another word. Duncan turned to say something to her and she slammed the door closed. "Those useless bastards!" she shouted as she paced furiously around the living room. Pacing, she remembered Ronin's instruction to make sure that her phone was on. She remembered that she had turned if off earlier that day to conserve the battery. The cell phone powered on as she walked into her bedroom to plug it into her charger. The phone beeped, indicating that she had messages. Aaliyah retrieved the charger, pushed the voicemail button and headed back to the living room. Just as she plugged in the charger she heard:

"You have twenty-three new messages." Aaliyah put the phone to her ear and listened. The first five messages were from friends frantic to find out how she was. The sixth message was from Jayden's brother, Stephan. He was unaware of the day's events; he was calling to inform his brother that the Army was going to stop loss him. This meant that even though his contract was done, the Army would be keeping him against his will. The next message was from Jayden.

"...Our house isn't safe" was the statement that stood out the most. She was too overwhelmed from hearing his voice.

Aaliyah's first thought was to run out and stop the negotiators from leaving. Her second thought was to call Ronin. Aaliyah took two steps toward the front door, when she heard a noise coming from the back of the house. She stopped and listened. Although she didn't hear anything else, she decided to go and investigate. She walked through the kitchen and headed for the back door, but froze in her tracks when she saw two shadows through the back door. She turned to sprint for the front door. Aaliyah got in three strides before the back door opened. She turned back around and ran into a wall screaming as she bounced backwards. As she sat on the ground, she saw two sets of legs in front of and beside her. She did not look up as she extended her leg and tried to land a kick to one of her assailants. Before she could get her leg fully extended, a hand reached down and stopped her. She looked at the hand around her ankle and started to scream. Another hand quickly covered her mouth. Her eyes widened in fear as she followed the hand around her ankle up to her assailants face. She gasped and became rigid when she recognized Jayden and her eyes got a little wider.

"Hey baby," Jayden said, looking down and smiling. The hand over her mouth belonged to Kristoff. Aaliyah stared at Kristoff with terror still gripping her. "You won't scream," Kristoff told her as he stared into her eyes. Aaliyah's pupils stopped dancing. "I won't scream," Aaliyah mumbled beneath his fingers. Kristoff removed his hand from her mouth and lifted Aaliyah up by her shoulders.

"Don't do that to my wife."

Jayden stepped between the two and shook Aaliyah from her trance. She shifted her gaze to Jayden. Aaliyah stared at him for five long seconds and then lunged and wrapped her arms around his neck. She placed kisses all over his face. "Oh my God, I missed you. I thought you were dead."

"I missed you too baby." Aaliyah hugged him tight for one full minute and then pushed him away. She surveyed his body up and down in amazement. "What the hell happened to you?" she asked.

Jayden held out his arms and turned so that she could see the entire physical transformation.

"You like?" he asked, smiling.

"You look incredible," Aaliyah answered as she continued to look at him in amazement.

"This is Kristoff," Jayden said as he pointed to the other man in the room. Kristoff extended his hand, but Aaliyah couldn't take her eyes off of Jayden.

"It's a pleasure to meet you," Kristoff said with his hand still extended. Aaliyah nodded in acknowledgment but never extended her hand. Kristoff pulled his hand back. Aaliyah stepped closer to her husband. Aaliyah started to cry and buried her face in his chest. "Who killed my babies?" Jayden hugged her tightly with his eyes closed, but that couldn't stop the stream of tears. Aaliyah cried hard and Jayden held her as Kristoff looked on.

Aaliyah's mind was racing; her mouth was too, between tears and sobs. "What happened in the garage? Who killed my children? Who picked you up?"

"I think you should sit down, Aaliyah. I have a lot to tell you and honestly, some of it is unbelievable," Jayden instructed as he helped her sit down on the couch. Jayden sat down next to her. Aaliyah's pupils danced between a smirking Kristoff and Jayden.

"Our children were killed by vampires."

"What?" she screamed in utter disbelief.

Kristoff looked around the living room before taking a seat himself. "This is going to be interesting."

"Listen, this is going to be hard enough. I need you to hear me out. Like I said, it's unbelievable," Jayden told her. Aaliyah glared at Jayden in response.

Jayden nodded his head and then continued.

"The people that killed the kids were vampires. They said that I had something that belonged to them. They were about to kill me when Kristoff saved me. Are you following me?" Jayden asked.

"I think so, but honey vampires don't exist," Aaliyah stated as she peered at her husband in disbelief.

"Yeah, well that's what I thought too. Let's just say I know for a fact they do exist and they killed our children."

"Who is this guy again and how do you know him?" Aaliyah asked, gesturing at Kristoff.

"His name is Kristoff, he's the guy who saved me and he's a vampire," Jayden said. Aaliyah slid to the opposite side of the couch, away from Kristoff. Staring at Kristoff for a few seconds, she raised an eyebrow at her husband.

"You had me going honey, for a minute there I almost believed he was a vampire."

Kristoff smiled back at her and then flashed his fangs. Aaliyah ran for the front door, startled. The negotiators were still parked outside when Aaliyah came running out of the house. They both looked up after she cleared the front porch. "Is everything OK Mrs. Endsley?" Duncan asked.

Aaliyah stopped and gaped at the officers and then back at her open front door. "I, I... I thought I... There, there..." she stammered. Duncan began walking towards Aaliyah when she came to her senses. She put her hands to her face and began crying uncontrollably, "They took my babies!" she screamed.

Duncan stopped a moment and then continued on toward Aaliyah. Duncan put his arms around Aaliyah and said, "There, there. We know it's tough and we're going to do everything we can to find your husband." Aaliyah played the role for another couple of minutes and then headed back to the house, thanking Duncan for the comfort. Kristoff and Jayden were staring at her when she came through the door. She closed the door, but remained close to it. With her back to the door, she stared at Jayden, then at Kristoff for several seconds before speaking. "Are you sure you want to stick with the vampire story, honey?" she asked, still shifting her gaze from Jayden to Kristoff.

"It's the truth baby, I promise," Jayden assured her.

"Let me try?" Kristoff asked. Aaliyah stared at Kristoff as if she was trying to figure him out. "Everything your husband told you is true," Kristoff started. "The kids were killed by vampires. I'm a vampire and so is your husband."

Aaliyah turned her head quickly and stared at Jayden with skepticism. "It's true baby, that's where this physique came from. I'm a vampire," Jayden told her. Aaliyah fell to the floor crying.

"God, what's happening to me?" she sobbed with her head in her hands. Jayden walked over to her and helped her up.

"There was no other way, honey," he said as he helped her to her feet. "Come on and sit back down, please." Aaliyah was losing it. She sat down and stared at Kristoff and he stared back at her. It took more than an hour for both men to finally convince Aaliyah of the story they were telling. However, once they had convinced her, they hit her with a bomb-shell. Jayden grabbed his wife's hands, kissed them and began.

"Aaliyah, you made a vow to love me until death do us part. That vow has been fulfilled; I am no longer human. My heart beats, but it isn't what's keeping me alive. I love you more than I ever have and I am asking you now if you would be willing to trade the rest of your days as a human woman to live and love me as an immortal."

"You mean as a vampire?" she interjected.

"Well, yes." Jayden responded.

"Let me get this straight. This guy is a vampire. You're a vampire. And you want me to become a vampire?" she asked with incredulity.

"…In a nutshell," Kristoff added.

"Why would I do that, even if it is true?" Aaliyah asked.

"I haven't given you all the details about the vam-pires that killed Brian and Jenny, but this man has promised to help me get them. And with your help we can avenge the kids," Jayden assured her.

"Can't you do it without me?" she asked.

"I'm sure I could, but I'm thinking about the big picture here," Jayden replied.

"You gotta give me some time with this one," Aaliyah told him.

"Time is something that we don't have a lot of," Kristoff told her. Aaliyah glared at Kristoff menacingly.

"Who the hell do you think you are? You show up here telling me my family are either dead or vampires, now you want me to just say, 'Okay, go ahead and bite me'? You sir, are out of your mind."

"Madam, I am the vampire who saved your husband from joining your children in the afterlife. I am the one who gave him a second chance at life. I am the one who is offering to help avenge your family. That is who the hell I am. Now take a moment if you require it."

The men let Aaliyah think about the situation a few moments.

"Where's the book?" Kristoff asked staring at Jayden.

"I think we need to get my wife situated first," Jayden replied.

"Will l I have to drink blood? Ugh, the idea of drinking blood is sick. I don't even like my steak medium rare," Aaliyah interjected, breaking her silence. Jayden shot a glance at Kristoff.

"Blood is the currency of our realm. It is necessary," Kristoff chimed in.

Jayden interjected, "If you say no, I will have to leave you. I won't jeopardize what little family I have left. But I am going after the bastards that took our children."

Aaliyah grazed her hands over Jayden's face. He looked younger.

"Of course I want to be with you, baby. But…but what about Katie and the life we have now?"

"We'll decide that together. Are you ready?"

"Do we have to do it right now? What about Katie?" she continued.

"Where is Katie?" Jayden asked, suddenly aware that she wasn't around.

"She left with James. He got her out of the house and away from the drama and me," Aaliyah told him.

"Good, it would be nice to have you help talk her into it," Jayden said.

"Back to the point at hand," Kristoff said, interrupting them. "Yes we have to do it now." Aaliyah frowned at Kristoff's insistence. Jayden explained what it would be like. He told her of the transformation he went through only a few hours ago.

"Will my body be like yours?" she asked, measuring her husband.

"Um, you would experience similar changes," Jayden told her.

Aaliyah stared at both men for several seconds before she spoke. "What the hell, let's do it. What do

I have to do?" Jayden looked at Kristoff and asked if he would do the honors; he wasn't comfortable biting his wife. But he was getting awfully hungry. Aaliyah was shaking when Kristoff touched her head. "I hope it doesn't hur…" Aaliyah was saying as Kristoff bit into her neck. Jayden's mouth watered as he watched Kristoff take blood from his wife. Kristoff took a lot more blood from Aaliyah than he had from Jayden. After Kristoff had released his bite, he repeated the process he had performed on Jayden. Kristoff cut his wrist and allowed Aaliyah to feed, while Jayden watched in horror.

Chapter 11

Jayden's brother Stephan was standing at parade rest in front of his seated battalion commander. Stephan's team leader was standing right behind him when he said, "With all due respect, sir, this is bullshit." The American flag and battalion colors flanked the colonel.

"Lock it up, Sergeant. You are a soldier; this is what you do. You are not the first soldier to be stop lossed and you will not be the last," the colonel ordered.

"Sir, my niece and nephew were murdered back home yesterday. It's all over the news. I need to go home for the funeral," Stephan replied.

"You know the regulation, Sergeant Endsley. We are deploying in three days and none of your immediate family has died. You are not authorized to take emergency leave." The colonel was getting agitated with the sergeant.

"Sir, I was supposed to be discharged in one week and now I can't even be there for my family? I don't believe my request is unreasonable."

"I don't bend rules for anybody Sergeant."

"You mean like promoting female soldiers that run 'special errands' for you? Funny, the duty day ends at 1700 yet Sergeant Mendoza frequents your house till 2200."

"*At ease, Sergeant!*" the colonel shouted as his face turned red and he stood up quickly. "I will not

tolerate your insubordination. You are dismissed."
Stephan snapped to attention, saluted, executed
an about-face and marched out of the office. He
stormed past his team leader and out of the building. He put his patrol cap on and walked briskly to
his truck. His bag was already packed with the round
trip ticket to McCarran International Airport sitting
on top of the bag.

Chapter 12

James knew it wasn't the best idea he had ever had, but he thought a little fun was what Katie needed. "Are you sure you're up for this?" James asked as he pulled the truck in front of the large beautiful house surrounded by party goers.

Katie paused before answering. "Yeah, I need something to take my mind off everything."

James opened his door and walked around to the passenger's side and opened Katie's door. Katie hopped from the truck to the ground and took hold of James's hand. They walked slowly up the pathway to the front courtyard. There were several drunken teenagers nursing cups of beer and various liquors. Those not drinking were smoking pot as they milled around the front of the beautiful home.

A group of seven watched as James and Katie approached. "Hey!" they all shouted in unison when they recognized James.

"'Sup, guys," James said to no one in particular. Katie and James continued on to the front door. James opened the door and allowed Katie to walk through the door first. She stopped and looked around at the scene of dancing teenagers. Katie soon started bouncing her head to the loud hip hop music blaring from an unseen source. James slightly pushed Katie in the back to allow him to enter. He walked through the door and began bobbing his head as well. The two of them made their way through the crowd of dancing people and continued on to the dining room. Five teenagers were sitting at the dining room table playing a drinking game. Katie and James stopped momentarily to check out the game; the group was playing Quarters. James laughed quietly when saw one of his friends forced to drink four consecutive shots of tequila. After a little bit though, James had had enough and grabbed Katie's hand and led her to the back yard. James surveyed the back yard as he came through the door and noticed a keg of beer about twenty-five feet away. James tightened his grip on Katie's hand and inched his way through the shoulder to shoulder crowd. Several people greeted him on his way through. Katie enjoyed being with the popular boy. She felt important. James finally arrived at the keg, which was sitting on ice inside of a plastic trash can. A tall, lanky inebriated teenaged boy was dancing alone in front of the keg. Katie recognized the drunk boy– Carlton Swift, a senior from Valley.

"Ten bucks a cup, you know the deal, Waddilove," Carlton slurred without stopping his dance. James looked at the boy in disgust, "Ten bucks?" James handed him a five dollar bill and took two cups from the table next to the keg. "I guess you can't add too good J-dub," Carlton said as he glared at James's date.

Carlton leaned in to get a better look at Katie, "Oh shit. My fault dawg, I didn't know you had li'l Endsley with you. Go on then, you're cool." Carlton leaned in closer to Katie. "Sorry to hear about your brother, baby girl. That was real fucked up," he slurred in a serious tone.

"Thanks," Katie replied as she leaned backed from Carlton.

James poured two beers and handed one to Katie. Katie wasn't a drinker, but she raised the cup to her lips and drank. The brew was cold and bitter, but it seemed to help in keeping the tears at bay. She made a sour face as she raised the cup for a second drink. James led Katie towards a lit fire pit, where several youngsters had gathered. The two had gotten within listening distance of the group when James stopped. James had focused his attention in the direction of the back door, but Katie was listening to the group in front of her. Katie's ears perked up when she recognized the drunken voice of Brian's girlfriend, Jessica. "I bet Mr. Endsley had something to do with it. And that helpless bitch Katie probably knows more than she's telling." Samantha stated before taking another drink from the cup in her hand. Katie had only taken a few sips of beer, but the alcohol was already affecting her courage. "Is that right, you stupid bitch?" Katie snapped as she walked closer to Samantha from behind.

Samantha spun around quickly and saw Katie frowning at her. "Oh my God, Katie. I didn't know you were standing there," Samantha said apologetically.

"No I don't imagine you did, you stupid ho." Katie growled. James had never seen this side of Katie, but was impressed by what he saw. He held Katie's hand tighter, but allowed the exchange to simmer before leading her away from the fire pit and back into the house. James stopped just inside the door and started talking to one of the varsity cheerleaders. The girl told James she was glad he had come. James smiled excessively as he talked to the girl and seemed to be engrossed in the conversation. Katie soon became jealous and bored with their conversation. She suddenly had the urge to utilize the restroom. She wandered through the house until she found it. After waiting in the long line she was able to finally get in. When she was done, she washed her hands and stepped back into the fray. Looking for James, Katie was now standing against a wall right next to a large young man wearing a Las Vegas High School letterman jacket. Katie glanced up at the 6"3', 240 pound white kid and saw that the man-child was staring down at her.

"What's up, shorty?" he shouted over the music, as he got even closer to Katie.

"Nothing," she yelled back.

"My name's Erick, but errbody calls me Easy," he slurred as he extended his hand.

Katie hesitated before taking his hand. "I'm Katie," she replied hesitantly as she shook his hand. Easy was drunk and his size made Katie more than a little uncomfortable. She casually surveyed her surroundings looking for James, but Easy continued engaging her.

"Where do you go to school?" Erick asked as he reluctantly released her hand.

"Valley," she replied as she continued to search for James.

Easy was inspecting Katie's face intently. "I know this is gonna sound crazy, but ain't you that girl from the news?" he shouted.

Katie stared back at him a moment before responding. "Something like that," she answered back. Easy started to say something else, but Katie interjected. "Look, it was nice meeting you, but I gotta go," she said as she tried to walk off. Erick reached out and grabbed her arm, preventing her from leaving.

"Nah, I'm trying to talk to you sexy," Erick shouted drunkenly over the music.

"Let me go!" she screamed.

"Are you always such a bitch? Relax, let's go upstairs for a little bit."

"I said no, jerk," Katie screamed as she tried to pull her arm free. Katie cocked back her arm and threw a punch square at Erick's nose. He easily caught her hand and deflected the blow. Erick grabbed her by the throat.

"Just for that I'm getting what I really want." He pulled her close and grabbed her ass.

As she tried to scream she heard the sound of flesh hitting flesh. Her arm was suddenly freed from Easy's grip. James had landed a strong blow, dropping Easy to the ground. By the time Katie realized what was happening, James had mounted Easy and was delivering devastating blows to his head. Three boys who were standing nearby tried unsuccessfully to pull James off of Easy, but it was Katie who convinced James to stop the onslaught. James and Katie were asked to leave the party. James was still panting and enraged while they exited the front door.

"I'm sorry for leaving you alone," he said apologetically as they headed for his truck. James and Katie were crossing the street when a tricked-out Cadillac Escalade pulled up just as they stepped from the curb. The tinted passenger window rolled down and the barrel of a shotgun came out.

"I saw you beat my boy down." The gun-toting passenger snarled with his finger on the trigger.

James froze and Katie screamed as they looked at the gun wide-eyed. They raised their hands instinctively as they stood in the street. James looked at the driver and recognized him from around town, but he didn't know the boy with the gun in his hand. If the gun wielder was anything like the driver, he was a hard-core gangbanger.

"What, nothin' to say, all-star? I oughta lay your ass out right here, fool," the would-be shooter snapped. Suddenly they heard an abbreviated siren and saw the blue lights of the metro approaching from down the street. "I'll holla at you later, player," the shooter said as he simulated firing a gun at James just before the truck sped off. The police car stopped in front of the party house and the officers got out of their cruiser quickly. They were completely oblivious to what had just happened, but they did notice James and Katie standing a few yards away with arms raised. The police were there to break up the party, not to save the day. James reached out and grabbed Katie who still had her hands in the air and led her quickly to his truck.

* * *

Aaliyah opened her eyes, and the first person she saw with her new vampire eyes was Jayden. She grabbed his face and kissed him.

"I promise to love you for eternity … but I'm still not looking forward to drinking blood," she whispered. They walked outside together. Her eyes were the same shade of blue they had always been; however, they had changed. Jayden couldn't take his eyes off her.

"I didn't think it was possible, but you are even more beautiful than ever."

"You are ever the gentlemen, Jayden."

"Wanna try your new powers? You are immensely faster, stronger, and more flexible." Aaliyah let go of Jayden and leapt on to the roof of the house. Then she executed a perfect back flip from the roof. "Just imagine what I can do in bed now!"

Jayden snickered and went over the rest of the powers with her in about an hour. After they were finished, they all went back inside. Aaliyah was sitting on the floor by the fireplace playing with her fangs when Kristoff finally spoke up.

"If you don't mind my rudeness, where is the Book of Eternal Night?"

"Why does it matter?" Aaliyah responded.

"Well, you see, it is the only thing that keeps that dark coven looking for you. Once it is away from here, they will leave you alone."

"How did they even know it was here?" Jayden responded

"Drake's blood is bound within the pages. He is drawn to it. As am I. I suppose now is as good of time as any to explain everything to you. It would be easier if you had the book to show you, though."

"Wait right here," Jayden said. He sprinted upstairs into his closet. Hiding behind a picture of his family was a wall safe. The familiar picture stopped him in his tracks. He remembered the day that the picture was taken. He could still taste the cherry lollipop that his little girl insisted that they share. The bright red candy in Jayden's memory giving way to the blood red night that she was murdered before his eyes. Crimson tears of rage now clouded his vision. Instead of moving the picture and dialing the combination, Jayden punched his hand through frame and the door of the safe. The picture shattered into a million pieces. He reached inside and felt around until he had the leather-bound book. He ran his fingertips over the book and shut the safe. He brought it back down stairs and laid it on the coffee table.

Chapter 13

Kristoff walked to the wall of books alongside the fireplace. He grabbed a Bible and brought it to the coffee table.

"This is a book of your history," he said. Then he gingerly grabbed the Book of Eternal Night.

"This is our history. Many times our histories have crossed paths, yet humans remain oblivious. Most don't even believe in their own Bible; why would they believe in us?" He flipped through the pages of the book and opened the Bible to show matching texts at certain points.

"The most ironic thing of all is that your Bible tells of our beginnings, and still people don't believe in us. I will show you how we came to be. Let me preface that by saying this: in the beginning God created heaven and hell. Humans do not populate hell, demons do. God created man and beast. He also created creatures and beings that were left out of the Bible and were put in the Book of Eternal Night. Initially this book was called simply 'the Book.' As time moved on, Christian archeologists heard about the Book and dubbed it the Book of Eternal Night. Now listen as I read from your Bible.

"Genesis six, verses one through four: 'And it happened, when men began to multiply on the face of the earth, and when daughters were born to them, the sons of God saw the daughters of men, that they were good. And they took wives for themselves from all whom they chose. And Jehovah said, "My spirit shall not always strive with man, in his erring; he is flesh. Yet his days shall be a hundred and twenty years." There were giants in the earth in those days. And also after that, when the sons of God came in to the daughters of men, and they bore to them, they were mighty men who existed of old, men of renown.'

"This passage is saying that the sons of God—angels—came down to earth and had children with human women. Now if you look in our Book, you will see a passage that you don't see in the Bible.

'The Alpha chapter three, verses three through seven: 'And the sons of God were not the only ones who saw that the daughters of man were good. The sons of Satan took wives as well, and their offspring numbered as many as the offspring of the angels. It was when one of the offspring of the half-breed angels fell in love with the offspring of the half-breed demon that the first vampire child was born.'

"If I keep reading, it will tell of how God became angry with the entire act of crossbreeding and eliminated the angels and demons that first started it. However, he felt that the vampire children were not at fault, and he allowed them to live. These natural vampires, as they are called, are much more powerful than other vampires, yet they only live to be about one hundred years old.

"The archangel Michael was furious with the decision to let them live. He lived to kill in the name of God. If the truth be told, he only lived to kill. He had taken a human wife for a brief spell, and she left him due to his insatiable temper and abhorrent bloodlust. When she left, she was with child. Her child grew to be a giant. She never told him who his father was. He was as fearsome as his father was. When he took a wife, he had no idea she was a demon half-breed. She was as much royalty in hell as his father was in heaven. Her mother was the daughter of Satan himself. When it came to pass that these two had a baby vampire child, it was unlike any other vampire. Its beauty was unsurpassed. The child grew very slowly. In fact, it was some three hundred years before the child reached puberty. The older he got, the slower he aged, until he stopped aging all together when he appeared to be about thirty years of age. This vampire had the ability to inflict normal humans with vampirism. He still lives to this day, but he remains hidden from everyone.

"About a hundred years ago, a man found this book and read that very story. He picked the parts he liked and embellished others and wrote his own book based on that one vampire. The man was a drunken Irishman whom many would say was a raving lunatic. His name was Bram Stoker. The vampire was the one you know as Dracula. He has had many names over the years and hasn't gone by that name in centuries. But please don't be mistaken, he is very real. He is your father and mine." Jayden raised his hand to pause the story.

"Wait, I am a historian, and I am fairly sure that the story of Dracula is based on Vlad the Impaler," Jayden said.

"Yes, and you also think that Jesus was a mortal man here on earth."

"Excuse me, but I don't appreciate your questioning by religious beliefs," Aaliyah said.

Kristoff smiled and touched both books again before continuing. He was making sure he used the right words.

"Before tonight you did not believe in vampires. Let me ask you, now that you are a vampire; do you believe in us?"

"Of course," Aaliyah replied.

"What did Jesus say at the last supper when he handed around a cup of wine?" Kristoff asked. Jayden's face fell when he replied, "This is my blood, drink it and have everlasting life."

Kristoff continued, "And what happened to Jesus three days after being crucified and speared?"

Aaliyah replied, rather shaken, "He rose from the dead."

Kristoff rose from his chair and walked to the sliding glass door and opened it. He stepped out to the edge of the pool. The water was glowing from the pool light. His hair was billowing softly in the breeze. Kristoff barely raised his voice so that it would carry into the living room.

"And lastly, what did Jesus do when his disciples were on the lake in a storm?" Without waiting for an answer he stepped off the ledge of the pool and onto the water. His foot never broke the plane of the water, and he began to walk across the water to the other side. Jayden and Aaliyah stood up together and walked to the pool to see this up close. Kristoff held his hands out at his sides momentarily and did a small spin for display. He then proceeded to walk back to them. He stepped back on to the ledge and guided the awe stricken couple back into the house.

"All immortals cannot do what I just did. It takes centuries to perfect and a few spells from the Book."

"Are you saying that Jesus Christ was a vampire?" Aaliyah questioned.

Kristoff merely smiled. Ignoring her question he said, "I apologize. I have digressed from the story I was telling you. Now where was I? Oh yes, natural vampires. It is extremely rare to find a natural vampire anymore because the only way they exist now is if two vampires make love and have the child. More often than not, though, it doesn't happen because the mother vampire can terminate a pregnancy simply by drinking any blood type other than the type she was born with. But that is just another part of our history. As with the hybrid children, vampires began to overpopulate the earth. They were slaughtering humans by the millions. To keep the vampire population in line, man was given certain people with powers: witches, warlocks, and shaman. These people have the ability to utilize magic and with it, kill vampires. Unfortunately, while they were revered in the days of the pagans, since the time of Constantine the Great they were discredited and killed. Because man is so evil, only one hundred witches and warlocks can exist at any given time."

"Wait, your saying witches exist?" Jayden asked.

"As do werewolves, stigmatics, and zombies," replied Kristoff.

He flipped some more pages, "Ah here is a story you might find interesting.

"Spells and sorcery chapter one, verses three through five: 'When a person dies, his spirit roams free in the universe. If the correct incantation is spoken, this spirit can be directed into a vessel. That is how the undead can walk the earth again. These are mummies. However, if the spell is done incorrectly, the vessel will be corrupted, and the spirit will not be able to control it properly. It will appear to move slowly and seem incoherent. These are zombies. If a demon realizes that a vessel has been opened with an incantation and the spirit cannot control it, it will force the spirit out and take over. At this time, the zombie will go into a rage and kill or infect everyone around it. These rage demons are not immortal and can be sent back to hell by decapitation.'"

Aaliyah looked up at Kristoff. "If what you are saying is for real, then the spirits of my children are roaming around the universe? Are you also suggesting that I can have my children back?"

"Yes, but it is quite complicated."

"Let's do it now," she exclaimed

"We cannot for quite some time. There are many prerequisites that include a shaman or sorcerer. Not to mention, if you do it incorrectly, you may damn their souls to eternal slavery in the pit or, even worse, zap them right out of existence."

Aaliyah exhaled and put her face in her hands. "I just want my babies back."

Kristoff held the book up and examined it. "The good news, I suppose, is that the first key to bringing your children back is this piece of literature." Kristoff said.

Light filled the living room as James pulled the truck into the driveway. James helped Katie out of the truck and they headed toward the house.

"What do we tell Katie?" Aaliyah asked Jayden.

"The truth," He replied.

James walked in the door first.

"I can't believe that asshole. He is going to get his someday. I'm sorry for leaving you alone, Katie." Katie and James stopped dead in their tracks when they saw Jayden. All three adults stood up.

"Coach, I'm so glad you're okay."

"Thank you James. I'm okay, and I'll call Ronin in the morn—"

"Better make it tomorrow evening," said Jayden. Why don't you go home James and get some rest"

"Yes sir," James turned around and walked out of the door.

Aaliyah whispered to Jayden, "I can't believe that little flirt trick works."

"We have got to give it a better name later because 'flirt' doesn't work for me," Jayden replied.

Katie ran up to her father and threw her arms around him.

"Daddy, I was so scared. I didn't know what happened to you. Where have you been? Who is this guy?"

Jayden and Aaliyah sat her down and explained everything that happened. When they were done, Katie stared at them in disbelief.

"Swear to God you are vampires!" she exclaimed. "Ok, do something vampirish." Jayden looked at Aaliyah, and they both descended their fangs.

"Holy Shit," she yelled

"Don't let me hear you curse like that, young lady," Jayden scolded.

"Dad, you drink blood; surely I can curse," she retorted.

"So the question your mother and I must ask you is this: do you want to join us? We will be more than a coven. We will be a family."

"Hell yeah!" she said. "Are you kidding me? That is awesome. Dad, look at you. You could be a fire fighter calendar model, and Mom, you could pose for Maxim. I definitely want it."

"Not tonight," Kristoff said. "The night is nearly over, and I must feed before I can do the dark trick again. This brings me to my next point. We must hunt now."

Jayden said, "I won't leave my girl here alone. Kristoff, please grab the book. Aaliyah, get the car keys. Katie, get some clothes and stuff for school. We will drop you off before we hunt."

"Where, Dad?"

"How about a penthouse? Wait, before we go, tell me what happened at the party that James felt the need to apologize."

* * *

Drake sat patiently in a dark room in a seedy motel outside of downtown Vegas.

Next door he could hear Pagan having some seriously sadomasochistic sex with Natalie and some hooker that was unfortunate enough to have been picked up by them. She thought her pimp was waiting for her outside, but Drake had made a quick meal out of him. The moaning next door got louder until a scream pierced the air. It was quickly muffled. The sound of something being shoved in her mouth muffled her screams. Drake could only imagine what that something was. The sound of flesh being ripped and bones snapping followed. Drake wondered why Pagan insisted on being such a messy eater.

Alexis opened the door with a metal key, further proof that this place barely qualified for a half-a-star rating. She walked seductively to Drake, a bottle of wine in her hand. She straddled him and opened the bottle. She took a huge swig of the wine and pushed it into Drake's mouth. Her lips mashed against his with desire. Drake wrapped his arm around her. He took the bottle from her. How thoughtful, she had filled it halfway with blood. Bottled blood was the worst and was only useful if you were on a ship or airplane. However, when mixed with alcohol, it was nothing shy of delicious. Drinking blood from a drunk person had the same effect. But getting this concoction brought to you by your lover, while ripping her clothes off, was priceless.

* * *

Jayden watched Kristoff hunt a couple south of the strip in an area that was not densely populated. It was simple. He walked with the couple to their nearby time-share. Then he managed to convince the husband to stand there and watch as he drained his wife. After he bit the man, he called Aaliyah over, and it took some convincing, but as soon as she commenced, she couldn't stop. Once they were done, it was Jayden's turn.

Jayden headed to the hospital. If the story his daughter told him was true, then the boy who was beaten must have been taken to the hospital. He gave the nurse his daughter's description of the guy who would have assaulted her. The nurse had no problem divulging that information to Jayden. Jayden ran full speed to the boy's house. Kristoff and Aaliyah showed up moments later. Jayden could smell the alcohol from the street. He knew he was asleep up stairs.

He contemplated the best way to do this. He could carve a circle of glass out of the upstairs window with his fingernails. He would lightly hop down from the window and stand over the half-naked boy. The room would be a pigsty. Clothes and food piled high. He wouldn't want Erick to miss this, though. How many fathers get to inflict true vengeance on a would-be rapist? Jayden would drag his nails across Erick's chest, Erick's eyes bolting open. Jayden would shove a dirty sock in Erick's mouth. That was one possibility tonight. But the thought of this scumbag wanting to rape his only remaining daughter caused Jayden to rage. His face disfigured with malice. His eyes crystal, bloodlust consuming him, Jayden dropped his fangs as low as they would go.

He leapt to the second floor window. He roared with all his might and sent the window exploding into the room. Erick screamed from his bed as he pulled the sheets to his chin like a child. Jayden could smell the fear emanating from the boy. He lunged at the boy, grabbing Erick by the throat and lifting him into the air. The mirror behind Erick caught the reflection of Jayden's face. Jayden stared at it for less than a second, but the fierceness of his face made it look completely alien to him. However, in that second, Jayden embraced his newborn heritage. He could feel the power of the angels and the savageness of the demons. He let it fill him until it was pouring out of his eyes. Erick was hanging terrified in Jayden's grip. Jayden let out a roar that shook the foundations of the house and set off car alarms in the street. Mirrors shattered all around the room, and blood began to seep from Erick's ears. Jayden then went for the jugular like a lion with a wounded antelope. He was in a feeding frenzy. He was draining Erick extremely fast, but to him it seemed like a drinking fountain that had poor water pressure on a hot summer day. As the last pint of blood rushed out of Erick's flaccid body, the door to the room burst open revealing Erick's mother.

A single mother on every government aid who worked two jobs so her son could wear his Nikes and jerseys, Natalie Le Beaux was exhausted. Her son had come home drunk and beaten. His two best friends, Rodney and Davis, brought him home from the hospital. She knew that these boys were bad news, and she was fairly certain that her son was in a gang with them. But she also knew that they were extremely loyal to her son and would do anything to help her family. She knew the money they gave to Erick was drug money, but when you have nothing, you don't look a gift horse in the mouth.

As she lay in bed, the room started to shake like an earthquake. The windows in her house were shattering around her. She said a quick prayer and ran upstairs. *Not another terrorist attack, please Lord.* She pushed open the door to see her son's body in the grip of a monster. He flung Erick's lifeless body out of the second story window frame. Before she could scream, she was in the clutches of this massive beast. His face was suddenly peaceful and soft. He was very handsome and spoke quietly to her.

She had forgotten why she came up here in the first place. What was he saying? Her son was over at a friend's house, and everything was okay. But hadn't she just seen something horrible? No, he was reassuring everything was okay. Of course it was. This man must be an angel. He was holding her so tightly. He nuzzled his face in her neck. He smelled like a spring day back down south. She closed her eyes and let herself go with a wonderful feeling. So many colors filled her brain until everything faded to black.

Jayden placed the dead body of Natalie La Beaux on the floor and let himself out of the back door to avoid detection by all the neighbors, who were out on their lawns surveying the damage.

Chapter 14

Drake sat at his laptop computer terminal, waiting for the webcam to show the figure on the other end. This coffee shop was open twenty-four hours a day, just like everything else in Las Vegas. When the face appeared, Drake smiled. The volume was cutting in and out, so they decided to type in the chat window.

Drake: So it appears the internet in your country still leaves something to be desired.

Tariq: So it would seem, Brother.

Drake: So let us cut to the chase. I have located "The Book." It is only a matter of days until it is in my possession.

Tariq: I am happy for you. But I cannot come. I have lived far too long to care about the rituals and history. I have seen history develop myself.

Drake: But, Brother, I need your help. It would appear that it lies in vampire hands.

Tariq: Then what's the problem? Simply ask to see it. It is not an uncommon courtesy to show another vampire.

Drake: It's complicated. Plus there is another issue. Kristoff is back.

Tariq: I don't want to come to America. They are destroying the country I live in. They treat the locals worse than I do. At least I offer them a peaceful death. They hate what they do not understand and kill indiscriminately. I do not care about politics, and even less about war, but one cannot respect a killer with no code. I can hear them bombing over the mountains. I feel sorry for them the day they come across me.

Drake: Enough, I know that I yield no power over you, Brother. You are my equal, and I respect that fact. But the bottom line is that the coven needs you. I need you.

Tariq: Fine, I will come in two months time. But I will not partake in your mindless killing, Pagan's blood baths, or anyone's public slaughter. I come for the Book and to deal with Kristoff. Then I will return to the Middle East.

The internet connection went out and the screen went black. The face reflecting in Drake's monitor had a smile from ear to ear.

Stephan walked in the front door of Jayden's house. The door was locked, but as usual, he had the key. "Hey everyone I'm home." *Where is everybody? It's noon on a Sunday. Jayden almost always watches the NFL games in the morning.* He heard a car door close. The door opened behind him.

"Uncle Stephan!" Katie ran and jumped into Stephan's arms.

"Hey there, little peach, where's my brother?"

Katie pulled away from Stephan.

"You're going to want to sit down Uncle Stephan." Stephan let his green duffle bag drop from his shoulder. He hopped over the back of the sofa and plopped down on the seat. Katie stood with her hands on her hips "So here's the deal ..."

James opened his eyes to the sound of a vacuum. He reached toward his nightstand and grabbed his cell phone. There were four missed messages and two text messages. One was from a cheerleader at his school, and one was from an NCAA football coach. He used to get excited when he would get letters or phone calls from the various coaches, but it has gotten old fast. He didn't really know where he wanted to go to college. Definitely a party school, but also one where the prospect of a national championship was likely. He put the phone to his ear to check his messages, deleting them one after the other until he got to the end. He still had two saved messages. He didn't remember what they were, so he listened to them before deleting them.

The last message was from Brian. James closed his eyes, and a tear ran down his cheek. It was nothing more than Brian calling to remind him to bring his letterman jacket that James had borrowed for a girl he had taken home. James clicked the phone off and rolled out of bed. He lumbered to the door of his bedroom. The vacuum cut off. James stretched his muscles and opened the door. The woman standing in front of him took off her cleaning gloves. James looked around the living room. It was spotless. The kitchen had been sanitized, and the whole house smelled like pine sol. The woman blushed at the sight of James. He realized he was only wearing boxer briefs.

"Where's my father?" James asked, rather bewildered.

The woman merely looked back at James.

"I'm back here, Son," Ronin's voice sounded from the backyard.

James walked to the backdoor. He could see the grill smoking as he neared the door.

"Dad, are you grilling this early in the morning?"

"Yeah, I got a call from Aaliyah last night; she said they were coming over tonight. I figured I'd make dinner. You know kind of a celebration that Jayden was found."

"So why are you cooking so early?"

"Well I'm deep frying a turkey for dinner, and I'm making ribs for lunch for both of us."

"Okay, it's just you haven't been this proactive when it comes to planning meals in a while," James said.

"I know, but with the loss of Brian I realized I'm only going to have you with me for another year, and then I won't see you for a long time." Ronin was never this emotionally available, and the mention of Brian made the situation a little uncomfortable.

"Dad, I'm not going anywhere for a while, but thanks for cooking. You haven't grilled since … well, since mom left. Speaking of which, who is the woman cleaning the house?"

"She's a lady I met at the bar last night. I gave her some money to straighten up the house."

"Dad, she doesn't speak English, and you don't speak Spanish. How the hell did you make these arrangements?"

"Son, three things in this world are universal: sex, money, and alcohol."

"Wow, Dad, you got a lady drunk, slept with her, and paid her to wash your clothes?"

"Something to that effect," Ronin remarked as he took a sip of beer.

"That's kind of scumbag move there pops, but I guess if it works ... "

"So you think that's a scumbag move huh? Let me tell you what a scumbag move is, Son. Walking out on your family on your son's thirteenth birthday because the guy you are screwing is moving to Seattle. Never calling me or so much as writing your son because you tucked tail and ran. I let you do what you want, Son. I never give you grief for letting girls stay the night, and I don't complain about anything really. But remember that I have raised you by myself for years now, and I never have had time to date. To be honest, I wouldn't know what to say to a woman at this point in my life. I figure a serious relationship is out of the question now, so please don't begrudge me a one night stand."

James stared at his father in awe. Ronin never mentioned his wife leaving him. He certainly didn't have blowups like that. James considered what his father said. He never really thought that the reason his dad never dated was because of him. He always thought his dad was too busy being a teacher, coach, and sports fanatic. He was under the impression his dad loved being a bachelor. He was always the life of the party or barbeque. He would have never considered that his father was lonely. James swallowed hard and took a seat on the green patio set.

Ronin stared at the food on the grill. The food required no flipping, but he did it anyway to busy himself. Then he asked, "So are you ready for the state championship? Do you think we should start Ford or Sims at defensive back since we've lost Brian?"

"It doesn't make much of a difference, Dad, they are both pretty good, but they are no Brian Endsley," remarked James.

"I know, Son, I know.

"So let me get this straight, Katie. Your brother and sister were killed by vampires. Your dad was kidnapped by vampires and made one of them. And tonight you will be made into a vampire." Katie nodded her head and looked for a reaction from her uncle. Stephan let out a huge laugh and kept it up until his sides hurt. Katie looked bewildered.

"What's so funny?"

Stephan slapped his knee as he stood up. "Little girl, you are suffering big time from post traumatic stress disorder. Welcome to the club. Now seriously, where is Jayden?"

Katie was furious. Why wouldn't he believe her? She was never prone to lying or making up stories. Stephan tapped his foot waiting for an answer.

"Fine" she said, you want to know where he is, I'll tell you. Dad and Mom are upstairs in their room. I don't recommend you wake them. And definitely stay out of Brian's old room."

"Yeah, and why is that?"

"Because Kristoff is in that room, and Mom and Dad might kill you if you disturb them. Haven't you ever read a vampire novel?"

"I only read army field manuals and Dan Brown books, kid. When either of them writes a vampire novel, then I will know what you are talking about. This is crazy; I'm going to go get Jayden." Ignoring Katie, Stephan bounded up the stairs. He walked up to Brian's door. He tried to turn the handle, only to find it locked. He put his ear to the door and listened. As he expected; no breathing, no sound, nothing. Aaliyah must have locked the door because it was too painful to look in there. He turned and walked down the hallway to the double door at the end.

"Yo, Jayden! Aaliyah! It's your favorite brother Stephan. Come on, I only have twenty-two hours before I am considered AWOL. Put some clothes on and open the door." He turned the knob and found it unlocked. He opened the door enough to fit his head in.

"Hello?" It was pitch black in the room. The familiar metallic scent of blood hit Stephan's nose. He flipped the light switch to no avail. The shutters and blinds were closed, and Stephan couldn't see the cord to open them. He fumbled through his cargo pocket, pushing his knife aside, and pulled his military grade, surefire flashlight out. They called this little flashlight "pocket sunlight" in Iraq because it illuminated everything. He shined it on the bed and saw two adult-sized lumps under the blankets.

He shined the light around the room and saw the clothes covered in blood on top of the hamper.

He pulled out his knife, not knowing what to expect. He checked the bathroom and closet for anyone who might be in the room. Then he crept to the bed. It was so cold he could see his breath in the light. He pulled the blanket back slowly. As the soft light spilled on to the bed, he saw the corpses of his brother and sister-in-law.

His eyes wide open and unblinking, Jayden lay topless with blood smeared across his face and chest. Aaliyah lay there, identical to her husband, her breasts uncovered and smeared with blood. Blood matted her long hair. Stricken with shock, Stephan dropped his flashlight. The button hit the ground, and the room went black.

He reached down to pick it up. As he felt around for the light, he heard the bedroom door open and close quickly. He could hear someone in the room with him. He flipped his switchblade open. The person was standing so close to him he could feel their breath on his neck. Working on pure military instinct he threw a quick elbow to the person's jaw, then quickly spun the person around and drew the knife across their throat.

Chapter 15

"Please don't kill me, Uncle Stephan. It's me, Katie!"

"Goddamn it, Katie, what the hell is wrong with you, sneaking up on me like that?"

Katie dried her eyes with her sleeve. "Give me a second to recover please. And if it's all the same to you, can we take this conversation downstairs?" Katie whispered through her tears.

Stephan closed his blade and led the way back downstairs. Katie was composing herself momentarily, and when she was ready, she spoke, "Now do you believe me?"

"Either you have two dead bodies up there, or you are telling the truth," Stephan remarked.

"You have to believe me, Uncle Stephan, they are swear-to-god vampires."

Stephan began to entertain the idea that vampires could exist. Then he had to force himself to believe that those corpses upstairs were actually vampires. Plus he knew that Katie was no liar. He got up and went to the freezer. He reached in and grabbed a blue ice pack. He crushed it between his fingers as he walked back into the living room.

"Here, peach, put that on your jaw. You are already starting to bruise. I'm really sorry, but what would posses you to creep up on me like that?"

"I wasn't trying to sneak up on you. I haven't had the courage to go in there while they slept. I have read that vampires will kill you if you interrupt their sleep. They don't even realize what they are doing, and they kill you. When I realized you were hell bent on going in there, I figured I'd be safe if you were with me. I didn't know you would go all Rambo on me."

Stephan got up and grabbed his bag.

"Well I sure as hell am not staying here tonight. Let's get out of here."

Chapter 16

Natalie and Alexis awakened at dark. They arose in the darkness of the grimy hotel room in the same bed. Both Drake and Pagan were still asleep. Drake lay in the other bed; Pagan was slumped in a chair with empty beer cans strewn about. The girls put on their clothes and walked outside. They began to walk out of the parking lot and down the road. Alexis broke the silence first.

"Do you think that what we are doing is … evil?"

Natalie shrugged her shoulders. "I don't know. I don't really care. All I know is that Pagan and I are having the time of our lives."

Alexis remained pensive for a moment longer. "Drake is truly upset about something. He won't let that book go." She paused for effect. "He called Tariq, and now Tariq is coming."

"Well, at least the whole coven will be together again," Natalie replied.

"Come on, don't you feel any remorse at all for killing that family?" Alexis asked.

Natalie glared at Alexis, "That's what we do, Alexis. We kill people. Your man is the leader of this coven. How do you think he would feel about you acting like such a coward?"

Alexis raged immediately. She grabbed Natalie by the hair, pulling her head backwards. She stared down into Natalie's eyes.

"I have been on this earth centuries longer than you. I have killed countless warriors, and ended even more lives. If you ever mistake my internal conflict with cowardice again, I'll rip you to shreds in front of Pagan." Alexis released Natalie's hair. Natalie stood there, frozen with fear. Alexis's face went back to normal as she smoothed the front of her shirt down.

"It was nice talking to you; we should do this again sometime," Alexis said as she headed back toward the hotel room.

Jayden awoke with his wife as soon as the sun had dipped below the horizon. They headed downstairs to the living room where Kristoff was already waiting. Kristoff handed them the letter from Katie saying that she was out with her uncle Stephan. The three of them went into the night to feed. This time they drove to a hardware store where several day workers still lingered after their hard day's work. They used their uncanny powers of persuasion to get the men into the vehicle, and killed them, draining every last drop. They opened the door when they were done, and Kristoff pulled out a knife and stabbed the three men in the chest, took their wallets, and pushed the bodies out of the vehicle into the empty parking lot. He explained that he made it look like a robbery so that the police wouldn't get any ideas about vampires.

Aaliyah then said that she wanted to go to the cemetery to visit her children. Kristoff and Jayden tried to protest, telling her that the spirits weren't there. She stood fast to her decision, and the three of them drove to the cemetery. They parked outside the cemetery and walked to the grave markers of their children in the rose garden. Before they were in eyesight, they could smell the presence of two living humans. They pushed through the trees and saw Katie and Stephan sitting in front of the headstones talking softly. Stephan looked up and saw the three of them. He stood up and took a slightly defensive posture. Katie saw them coming now too and stood up. Stephan put his hand on Katie's stomach and pulled her behind him. Jayden saw this and smiled momentarily. He held his arms out inviting his brother. Stephan didn't move. Jayden told him that it was clear that Katie had told him of their transformation and the Stephan had nothing to fear. Stephan took a tentative step toward his older brother. He put his hand out and touched his hands in disbelief. As he did this, Kristoff had a flashback.

The dozen or so men were in the room when Jesus appeared. Thomas was reaching out to touch the holes in Jesus' hand. Thomas didn't believe anything unless he could see it. He didn't believe that Jesus had risen from the dead. Kristoff knew it was possible, though, because of the recent transformation he had undergone himself. Jesus looked up at Kristoff knowingly. He had somehow known Kristoff's transgression. He then gazed at the other guilty men but said nothing. It was all said within his stare.

Stephan walked around his brother and inspected him.

"Well, you're in great shape for being dead, I guess." He turned to Aaliyah and ran his hand through her hair. Then he softly tilted her chin up and pressed her top lip back. The razor sharp fang gleamed in the night. He turned back to Katie and gave her a somber look.

"I'm sorry for doubting you, girly." He gave her a hug before turning back to his brother. "So where do we go from here?"

Chapter 17

As the Endsley family drove back to the house, Kristoff sat next to Stephan in the back. Due to the lack of space, Kristoff was pressed quite tightly against Stephan. Kristoff's cold skin was icy, even through Stephan's sleeves.

"So let me ask the glaring question," Stephan said. "What do you guys plan on doing with Katie?" The silence in the car was deafening as the shame of doing what they planned made it difficult to say it aloud.

"Katie will become one of us," Jayden said. Katie pressed against the door and buried her head in her chest.

"Are you insane? You can't do that, Jay. Just think of the life you will deprive her of. She will never finish high school, never going to college, no husband, no children!"

Aaliyah retorted, "It is her decision, not yours or mine. Plus she will finish school online. She can marry if she pleases, so long as the man is willing to adapt to her … lifestyle."

"Let me understand this; she can marry a man who is willing to give up his life for her, is that about right? And what about kids?"

Aaliyah pressed, "Don't for one second think we haven't thought about that, Stephan. It breaks my heart, but not nearly as much as the idea of living

without her. Regardless, she can have children."
Aaliyah turned around to look at Kristoff.

"She can have a natural vamp … she can have a natural baby."

"Look, guys, I'm going back to the war, and I don't want to think about the possibility that Katie is out murdering people."

Changing the subject, Jayden asked him, "What part of the Middle East are you going to?"

"The part people don't come back from," Stephan responded solemnly.

Driving straight faced, Jayden replied, "Then you shouldn't go."

Laughing, Stephan replied, "And be sent to jail for going AWOL, no thank you."

Katie looked up from her quiet position at Kristoff and said, "Well can't you turn Uncle Stephan. That way he can't be hurt?"

"Absolutely not. I have no desire to be a Wes Craven movie character." Stephan interrupted. As they turned into their neighborhood, a hooded jogger was running down the street.

Chapter 18

James put his hooded sweater on and stepped out of his house. He turned his MP3 player on and put the earphones in. His breath was visible as he stepped off the porch. He loved this time of year. The crisp clean air made jogging so much more enjoyable. This weather would only last a few weeks.

Las Vegas doesn't have four seasons. The leaves on the trees don't change colors like New England. They die and fall off the trees in a matter of days. There is only summer and winter.

Today was one of the transition days between the two extremes. Even now, in the hours before dawn, James smiled and pulled the hood over his head. He turned the music up and headed down the street. He noticed the Endsley's vehicle passing as he ran. He kept trudging through the neighborhood. He began breathing evenly as his paced leveled out. He decided to run a new route as he was going. As he turned into a new neighborhood he hadn't run before, he stopped in his tracks.

He was staring at a house that looked like a hurricane had hit it in the middle of suburbia. The top floor of the two-story house looked like it had been hit by a rocket. There was glass everywhere, and the garage door had a split down it. The smashed Spanish tiles covered the floor like seashells. The whole scene was blocked off by police tape. The black SUV in the driveway began to back out as he took in the entire melee. As it reached the apex of its reverse, he looked through the window at the same gangsters that pulled a gun on him the other night. The two thugs inside recognized him instantly and pulled their guns out. James took off running. The large SUV was forced to do a U-turn in order to give chase. James ran though a front yard and hopped the wall. He ran through the back yard avoiding the large dogs that were barking at him and hopped a series of walls until he emerged on another street. He made sure the vehicle was nowhere to be seen, and he ran full speed back to his house.

As James got back to his house, he locked the door behind him and bent over, breathing hard. Ronin looked up from his computer screen at his son. James dismissed his father's concerned inquiry and headed to his room. He walked through the door and closed the door harder than he had planned. He slumped to the floor and started crying. The tears flowed from his very soul. It wasn't fear of the gangsters or of the guns they wielded that made him weep, it was the first time in his life that he acknowledged his own mortality. His tears shook his body through his sinewy muscles. He had always felt invincible. Now he felt that at any moment he could join his best friend in death. The thought of his best friend's brutal death only made him cry harder. The young man, who wouldn't flinch at the idea of a fight with anyone, was now sobbing like no one had ever seen.

Chapter 19

That evening Jayden, Aaliyah, and Kristoff awoke in the house. Jayden walked to the front door to find a box with a blinking light next to the handle. Katie walked out of the kitchen eating an apple.

"Uncle Stephan figured we needed better security installed after what happened to Brian and Jenny. He had the guy install a five-inch dead bolt that is activated by fingerprints. I already put mine in the system." She reached in her back pocket and handed Jayden a small pamphlet.

"Here are the instructions, Dad." Jayden breezed through the manual and opened the door. Within five minutes he had programmed his and Aaliyah's fingerprints into the system. He looked at Kristoff.

"You saved my life, and I feel a strange loyalty to you that I really can't explain. I want to give you access to our home." Kristoff walked to the door and imprinted his thumb. He had to do it several times for the machine to pick up his prints. He looked at his thumb.

"I am so old that my finger prints are fading." He closed the door and sat down on the sofa. "The attraction that you feel to me is natural. It is the same I have for my master and the same that Katie will feel for you when you turn her. You are more than a family now; you are a coven. You and Aaliyah will forever feel drawn to me, and I to you."

Katie was turning the propane up on the gas fireplace. The blaze grew large.

"Please, Kristoff, before I am turned tonight, tell me how you came to be what you are." Kristoff stared into the blaze for what seemed like forever. Katie opened her mouth to repeat herself when Kristoff began to speak. "What happened to me happened long ago, and I have never told the story. But to understand what happened to me, I must give you some backstory. Prepare yourself, because this story may shock you. This story takes place over two thousand years ago."

Chapter 20

33 A.D. Rome

The walk to the town had taken a toll on the weary travelers. In the time before vehicles, and when only the elite owned horses, walking was the preferred method of travel. The men had become accustomed to following their leader from town to town and even across blazing deserts. Once they had arrived at their destination, the men waited outside the motel owner's front door. Two of their party went inside while the others loitered patiently. The sun had set an hour ago and the heat still caused the sweat to roll down their faces, though their beards, and gather in their modest garments. The two men came back out with a key in their possession. The group headed back around the small complex of buildings. They opened the door to one of the larger rooms and entered. The room was filled with nothing more than a dining room table and chairs. On the table were a large loaf of bread, a sack of wine, and one large chalice. In the corner were two bowls filled with water for washing.

The men took off their dusty sandals at the door and filed in, taking seats at the table. One of the men walked over to the bowls of rose water and carried them from man to man washing their feet. The men were a little shocked because this duty was customarily reserved for the least among them. Jesus, however, was the leader of this group, and here he was humbling himself before his own men. When he was done, he cleaned himself up and poured the water outside the door. He walked back in and sat at the table. There were a total of fifteen men at the table. The few women who traveled with them were at the house of a woman they knew. It was not acceptable for women to spend the evening with unmarried men.

As Jesus sat down, he looked to his right at his childhood friends Tariq and Drake. The two brothers were talking amongst themselves. He had spent many summers with them, having fun and getting in trouble. He smiled as he recalled a time when they were seven or eight. The boys were playing on the rooftop of Drake's house. Tariq and Jesus were walking along the edges of the house trying to maintain their balance when Tariq slipped and fell from the roof. He fell through the air and landed on his neck. Jesus heard the snap of his friend's neck and scrambled off the roof to get to him. When Jesus got to Tariq's lifeless body, he was already surrounded by the villagers. The angry villagers were accusing Jesus of pushing him off the roof. People were already grabbing stones to hurl at Jesus. Jesus pushed his way through the angry throng of people and kneeled at his friend's side. Jesus closed his eyes and prayed to his father. Then he opened his eyes and yelled at the body of Tariq, "Tariq, wake up and tell these people I didn't push you!" Tariq's eyes fluttered open, and he sat up. He rubbed his neck where it had been broken, felt no pain. Jesus helped him to his feet, and he hugged Jesus. The angry mob dissipated quickly, and the people with stones let them fall to the ground.

Jesus then looked to his left, where his favored disciple Peter sat stretching his calves. He smiled as he thought about the storm in Galilee. The men were on the fishing boat, and the winds were tossing the boat in the frothy waters. Jesus looked out and saw some of the men begging for help. Some were begging God and others were actually calling out to Jesus on the shore. Peter on the other hand was pulling at the rigging and trying to right the boat. Jesus walked out from under the tree where he had been napping. He took in the situation and stopped to pray to his heavenly father. He walked out to the shore and walked out on the lake.

As Jesus walked out toward the fishing vessel, Peter noticed that Jesus was on the lake. Without regard for himself, Peter jumped overboard. When he landed in the water he must have landed on a sand bar, because he didn't sink at all. He landed on his knees and stood up. He looked down only to see there was no sand bar under him. In fact there was no land at all. He was standing on the water. His mouth dropped open, and he looked up through the storm at Jesus. Jesus was about a hundred feet away and called out to Peter. Peter could barely hear Jesus. Jesus was motioning for Peter to walk to him. Peter started walking in amazement toward Jesus.

He had made it about ten feet when a wave rolled across the water and smacked Peter. Peter took his eyes off Jesus for a second and began to sink immediately. Peter began to cry out to Jesus for help. Jesus raised his hands and quieted the storm and Peter swam to Jesus, who pulled him back on top of the lake, and they walked off arm in arm.

The man next to Peter had his head bowed and nervously scanned the room. He couldn't meet Jesus' gaze and seemed preoccupied with a crack in the wooden table. Peter slapped the man on the back. "What's the matter, Judas?"

Drake and Tariq looked up from their conversation. Judas shook his head and shrugged off Peter's hand. "I'm not feeling well from the journey," he replied.

"Why don't you go lie down in the bedroom then. We'll save you some bread," Peter remarked.

"I'm fine," Judas lied.

Jesus called the small gathering to order. He filled the goblet with wine as he spoke. He began to tell them that he felt their time together was coming to an end. The men began to grumble at this news, but Jesus silenced him with a wave of his hand. He scrapped his hand along the unfinished side of the wooden table, drawing blood. He allowed several drops to fall into the wine and held the goblet with both hands at shoulder level.

"This is my blood. Drink of this and have everlasting life. This will be a covenant between you and me." He passed the goblet to Drake, who stared at the goblet for several moments before taking it. He placed the chalice to his lips and drank deeply. He then handed the goblet to his brother, who followed suit. When Tariq handed the cup to the next person, they saw the blood residue along the rim and quietly passed it around the table. All the rest of the disciples did the same. They had never disobeyed Jesus before, but this seemed a tad extreme. When the goblet was passed to Peter, he kissed the cup, raised it over his head in thanks to God, and drank the rest of wine himself.

Jesus smiled at Peter and reached for the bread. Judas cried out before Jesus touched the bread, "My Lord, let me break the bread since your hand is bleeding."

Jesus displayed his hand, completely healed, to the table. He then broke the bread and handed it around the table telling them how this was his body. He would be broken like the bread. Drake interjected, "It will be a frosty day in hell before we let that happen." Jesus smirked at his friend and told him to be at peace.

Tariq didn't like the foreboding tone that Jesus was using. It made him uneasy. He wiped his brow, which was now perspiring, and wiped the sweat on his robes. His head started pounding, and his stomach was churning. He stood up slowly and excused himself. He walked to the bedroom and lay down. Seconds later, the door opened, and Drake walked in, followed by Peter. Peter said he must have had too much wine. He felt sick, as did Drake. Drake and Peter each lay down on the floor next to Tariq. The men could not scream; it felt as if their mouths were sealed shut and ice was running through their veins. The men in the other room left the house and headed to a garden. As the front door shut, the three men in the room began writhing in pain. As they rolled across the dusty floor, the ice in their veins began to move. It felt as though the ice was crystallizing in their hearts and spreading out through their bodies. As the icy sensation reached their eyes, the men stopped moving. The breath left their bodies, and the men began slipping into a state of hibernation, their eyes wide open, crystallized.

As the group of men walked from dinner, Jesus explained that the three comrades they had left behind would be fine. They continued up a small hill until they reached the gardens of Gethsemane. When they arrived at the entrance, Jesus left his men to guard it while he went in to pray. As the hours wore on, Jesus felt an intense fear, as he knew what was going to happen. He rose from his knees and wiped the tears from his face, accepting his fate. He walked slowly back toward his men, savoring the aroma of the bushes and lilacs. He could already hear the mob coming up the hillside. As he reached his disciples, he found them all sleeping. A part of him was enraged as these were his guards as well as his followers, but another part of him understood that they were only human, and the hour was late.

The light at the base of hill was growing with the din. The torches were held high, and Jesus knew his hour had come.

Jesus was brought in front of the Pharisees. These were Hebrew leaders with complete disdain for Jesus. He had embarrassed them on numerous occasions, proving that they were wicked and not good in the eyes of God. They had waited patiently to set him up and arrange his legal public murder. As they hurled insults and false accusation at him, Jesus stood steadfast and silent. He could still see in his mind his men waking up amongst the madness and scattering to the four winds. He knew that Peter would never have stood for that. He, Drake, and Tariq would have fought to the death ... a fight they now could not lose. The Pharisees bound Jesus' arms and forced him to King Herod's throne room, some ten miles away. King Herod had once tried to slay Jesus when he was an infant. It was foretold that the star that appeared above the manger Jesus was born in would usher in the King of the Jews. Naturally Herod took this as a slight, and a threat to his kingdom. He had his men search high and low to find this "King of the Jews," but alas for Herod, Jesus' mother hid him far too well for him to be found by the soldiers.

As Jesus walked into the decadent palace, he looked around to see exotic animals and people dancing and fornicating all over the throne room. Alcohol and wine flowed freely out of ruby encrusted chalices and into people's mouths. It was being poured across women's bodies and lapped at by men, women, and beasts. He was shoved hard from behind. He walked up the steps to the throne.

Herod sat upon his throne staring at Jesus. Herod asked if Jesus had anything to say for himself. Jesus remained mute. Herod then began to mock Jesus, calling him the king of nothing. "Surely this man is a carpenter, not a king."

Jesus kept his head down, hearing the insults but not responding. He flashed back to the garden where his trusted friend Judas kissed him on the mouth, betraying him to the Pharisees, and backed away quickly into the mob. He wondered if Judas even had the nerve to follow him to this sham of a hearing.

Herod signed a piece of parchment and handed it to the Pharisees. They smiled wickedly and led Jesus through the night to the high court of the Romans. When they arrived at sunrise, the head magistrate, Pontius Pilate, was already dealing with state affairs. They presented Jesus to Pilate and gave false testimony to him. They handed over the decree that Herod had signed. Pilate took the document and read it. It explained that while Herod could find no fault in Jesus, the Pharisees could start a revolution that would overthrow his kingdom and possibly challenge Rome. Pilate could not ignore this fact, as he had already put down three uprisings this year. He tried for several hours to persuade the Pharisees to let this innocent man go.

He knew that Caesar would have his head if he lost control of his province. He also knew that Caesar was to visit in two days. He arranged to have Jesus beaten; perhaps that would satisfy their bloodlust. The guards took Jesus away and flogged him mercilessly. His skin and flesh ripped from his body. The salt from his sweat and tears made it hurt that much more. After the savage beating, he was brought back to Pilate. His whole body ravaged and covered in blood, Jesus stood steadfast as ever. The Pharisees would not be satisfied with that, so Pilate washed his hands of this man Jesus and ordered that he be crucified. Jesus was taken to the top of a hill called Golgotha, and was crucified by the Romans. Two hours later, his heart stopped.

The next morning Drake, Tariq, and Peter were able to move. They got up from the floor and walked outside. Tariq, who had always had poor eyesight, realized that his vision was perfect. Drake wasn't wearing shoes, yet he could not feel the stones digging into his feet. When they told this to Peter, he laughed at them and told them that it must be due to the long restful sleep they had gotten. He went into the house to go get their sandals and returned out in a few moments. They were going to look for Jesus and the other men.

As they walked into the town, people were acting very strange. This town, which had been so kind to them before, was now standoffish and rude. Peter asked a man if he had seen Jesus, and the man ignored him and kept walking. Drake scratched his head and suddenly spoke up.

"Mary. We can go to the house Mary was at. I'm sure she knows where they are." The men walked to the home and saw that the windows were covered.

Peter knocked on the door. He could hear people in there, but no one would answer the door. He knocked again and shouted that it was Peter, Drake, and Tariq there to see Mary. Someone peaked through the window shade and moved to the door quickly. Mary opened the door and quickly ushered the men in. When they got in the house they saw that they were surrounded by the disciples. Peter smiled. He greeted the men and went to hug his brother Simon only to get told to be quiet. The smile left his face when he realized they had all been crying. Drake looked around the room.

"Where is Jesus?" he inquired. The men began to cry harder.

"I said, *where is Jesus?*" Drake shouted. Mary told the men what happened. Peter fell to his knees and said a prayer. Tariq's jaw dropped as he tried to process the tale. Drake however, turned his gaze on the disciples. He had never really cared for many of them. His sole interest was Jesus, his lifelong friend. Drake was spewing venom in their direction.

"You pathetic cowards! You allowed the son of God to be captured and killed! Not one of you was worthy to walk in his presence. I knew you were all worthless, and now you've proven it."

Peter stood up. He and Tariq seemed to agree with Drake's sentiments.

"You hide in here, afraid that you may be identified as his disciples. You should be proud to be his friends," Tariq said.

Peter whispered, "None of you were his friends. You let my master, my Lord, my closest friend in the world be killed. You are all weak and pathetic. There will be vengeance … there will be blood."

Drake roared at the top of his lungs and punched the wall. When he hit the wall, his hand went through to the other side. That wall was made of three layers of stone. There was no wood only mortar and brick. He pulled his unscathed hand back through the wall in amazement.

The disciples stared in awe.

Chapter 21

Drake stumbled out of the door into the daylight. Peter and Tariq followed, closing the door behind them. The three men walked in silence back to the room where they had spent the night. Once the door had closed, they sat at the table.

"Do you want to talk about what just happened in there?" Tariq asked.

Drake spoke softly, "I punched through a wall, and I felt no pain. Since I woke up this morning I feel better than I ever have in my whole life. I feel strong and focused."

"So do I," Peter said. "This must be the covenant that the Lord spoke of. The others were infidels and didn't drink of him. That is why we passed out so early."

Tariq spoke next, "I wonder what else we can do, if strength and good eyesight are the extent, or if there is more that comes with this covenant." Answering his own question, he slid his hand along the same jagged point on the table that Jesus had the night before. He was able to draw blood with a considerable effort. He held his hand over the candle in front of him. Four droplets of blood spilled from his hand, extinguishing the flame. When he turned his hand over, he had healed completely. Peter nodded his head in acknowledgement.

"So what are we going to do with this power?" Peter asked. Drake looked at him from across the table,

"Justice," Drake said with a straight face.

"No." Tariq smiled. "Vengeance."

Peter thought briefly that this isn't what Jesus would have wanted. He preached love and for-giveness. As if reading his mind, Drake said, "Jesus wouldn't have wanted to have been crucified. He didn't want to be flogged. And I for one will use these gifts to ensure no person is treated like this again. The question is who do we hold responsible? Who do we go kill?"

Tariq spoke loudly, "All of them. Anyone who helped tie him down, anyone who held a candle for them to read the lies off the parchment to have him condemned, and anyone who gets in our way. Plus I plan on a special death for the Pharisees, Herod, and Pilate."

Peter ground his teeth together and said, "And I will handle Judas." The men conspired at the table for three hours. When the sun was touching the horizon in the west, they marched to the temple. The temple was constructed of three parts. The out-ermost was a courtyard. It was a market where you could buy livestock to sacrifice. The next inner part was a place where all people could worship god and hear the teachings of Moses. The most inner sanc-tum was the most holy area known as the tabernacle. It was reserved only for the Pharisees. The three men walked up steps of the temple. The outer market was only populated by the greedy merchants who were overcharging the poor for a chicken, goat, or dove. They were counting their silver when the three men came up the steps. They were talking about the night before.

"Can you believe they paid us this much silver just to lie about that man?"

Another interjected, "I'm glad he got what he had coming to him. That piece of garbage came in here and over turned my tables and livestock. Who the hell is he to tell me I can't charge what I want to the poor. So I just embellished a little and told the Pharisees he stole my money and planned to revolt against the temple."

The three men crested the top step just as he finished his tale. They had heard every word. They stood at the top step with the sun setting behind them. A breeze blew their hair softly. All three had cropped off their beards. Their crimson tunics, representing the blood of Jesus, billowed softly.

For a moment there was complete stillness. The merchants stared at the three men. Peter ran his hand over the handle of his sheathed sword. Drake clutched at the dagger in his belt. Tariq held nothing but the fierce gaze of all the merchants. The merchants feared that these men meant trouble. Perhaps they were bandits trying to rob them. The dozen merchants pulled their swords and held their ground. Tariq said in an even tone, "Kill them all."

Drake lunged at the man closest to his and plunged his dagger deep into the man's sternum. Two merchants attacked Peter at the same time. Peter felt like he could see the men moving in slow motion. He easily avoided the swipes of the men's scimitars. He swung his sword at the first man, only to underestimate his own strength. He chopped the man's head off and his own momentum kept the sword swinging into the arm of his other opponent. He severed the man's arm. He pulled back his sword and plunged it into the one armed man's ribs. Tariq leapt across the room and grabbed two men by their throats, their swords clanging loudly on the ground. He lifted them off the ground and snapped both of their necks in his grasp. The remaining merchants tried to run, but the three men were far too fast and cut them down before they could reach the temple steps.

The merchant's bodies lay strewn across tables and on the stone floor. Blood ran down the steps of the temple like a river. The three men walked over the bodies and into the middle sanctum. Waiting there were Roman guards paid by the Pharisees to protect them. The guards were standing at attention. The captain of the guard had heard the commotion and had gone to see the mêlée. He now had his soldiers ready. The squad of twenty soldiers was formed and ready to fight. They were in a phalanx formation. The shields protected the front soldiers, while the soldiers behind wielded large spears. The three men stood at the door witnessing the military precision of the guard. The guard was a hundred feet away and began moving as one tight formation toward the men.

An idea suddenly came to Peter, but it wasn't his own. He had heard Tariq think of how to best take out the soldiers. Drake looked at both of them as he realized that they could hear each other thoughts. Since it appeared they were all on the same page, they waited patiently for the guard to move closer. The tips of the spears drawing ever nearer to the men, it was apparent that this phalanx had no shields for the men in the back. This cube of men advanced to within fifteen feet of the three, when Tariq and Drake sprung over the phalanx. It was an impossible jump by mortal men's standards. They landed behind the formation and began killing the soldiers. The soldiers in the back were wielding large spears that were too awkward for close combat. The phalanx immediately fell apart, and Peter ran into the rumble. Sword and bone connected repeatedly. The three men were on a rampage. The captain of the guard thrust his sword into Peter's back. Peter looked down at the steel blade sticking through his stomach. The captain pulled the sword out, yelling a victorious war cry. Peter, still looking at the hole in his stomach, watched it close almost immediately. He felt no pain and smiled at his good fortune. He spun around at the surprised captain and grabbed him by the ears. He pulled until his ears ripped off. Then he kicked him in the chest. The captain's heart stopped immediately. Peter sprung back into the fight, killing until the last soldier collapsed to the floor.

The three men walked toward the tabernacle doors. The doors were ten feet high and lockable from the inside. The oak doors had a large wooden bar that could be laid across the inside to keep out invading armies. The three men heard it fall into place on the other side of the doors. They could hear the whispers of the Pharisees on the other side. The three men counted to three and kicked the door with all their might. It splintered the security bar on the inside, and doors blew open. The six Pharisees were huddled in fear around the altar. The three men covered in blood advanced to the altar. They threw the Pharisees face up on the floor of the altar. Drake shouted them to shut their sniveling mouths. All three men had their blades out.

Tariq stood over the sobbing men. "Where is the betrayer? Where is Judas?

The Pharisees nearest Tariq lay trembling in fear.

"We do not know. He returned his thirty pieces of gold and shouted that he would die where Jesus died," the Pharisee shouted.

Tariq looked at Peter, who nodded in understanding that Judas would return to the place of the skull, where Jesus was murdered, to take his own life. It was a long journey, and the men had plenty of time to catch him. Tariq returned his attention to the Pharisees.

"For the lies you told against an innocent man, you shall lose the ability to speak." The men walked down the row, cutting the tongues out of the Pharisees' mouths. The priests screamed in agony. Drake screamed back at them, mocking their pain.

Peter spoke next, "For tying an innocent man up and having him struck you shall lose your ability to strike." The men cut off the hands of the priests next. The priests tried to struggle to no avail.

Drake spoke last, "And for arranging the death of our best friend, you will lose your ability to live."

The men nodded their heads and lined up along the row of Pharisees. Drake would cover the priest's mouth, forcing him to drown in his own blood while Peter and Tariq held the next priest's head up, forcing him to watch his fellow brother of the cloth die. They did this until every one of the Pharisees was dead. The men walked out of the temple over turning candles and grabbing the torches along the wall. The blood-soaked men set fire to the temple as they walked out into the night.

Chapter 22

As the men headed north to Herod's palace, they left bloody footprints in the dust on the roadside. As they closed in on the palace gates, they remained silent. When they came to the sentries at the gate, the sentries instructed them to halt. The sentries told them to announce their business. Peter told them they had an audience with the king.

"The king will not return until just before sunrise."

"Then may we wait for him inside?" Peter asked.

The sentry looked at the men's disheveled appearance. "You may not. You should not be unclean in the throne room. I tell thee that you must go clean yourselves before entering," the guard replied.

Tariq stepped forward toward the guard. He leaned in closely, "Then perhaps we shall bathe in your blood." He quickly reached for the guard's sword on his hip. He flipped it around in his hand expertly and ran the blade across the guard's throat. He picked up the body and tossed it into some shrubbery to conceal it. The men stormed the palace doors. Tariq shoved the double doors open and the men took in the same sight that Jesus did the previous night.

Hours later, when King Herod came home, he stopped his stallion at the gate. The guard was waiting for him. His head wrapped with a scarf, probably to keep the dust storms from ripping his face up.

The guard opened the gate and let the small entourage in. Herod crossed the gates threshold and dismounted the horse. He handed the reins to the guard, who followed and headed up the steps. The servants who entered with him must retire through the servant's quarters.

As he entered the doors into his throne room, the ruckus party that usually welcomed him was silent. The candles were all out, and the dim room needed a torch desperately. He looked at the women who were in seductive poses with men on top of them. He looked at the tigers that were chained to the marble pillars, apparently asleep. As he walked slowly toward his throne, he glanced at the chambermaids, who seemed to be kneeling as though they were cleaning. His palace guard was leaning against the wall, seemingly intoxicated. No one was moving, and everyone was silent. As he approached the throne, he stopped at his wine station to poor a wine from the sack, since his wine slave was nowhere to be found. He was very thirsty from his travel and gulped the wine quickly. He immediately spit it out. It had gone horribly bad. Someone would be whipped for this. Suddenly, a laugh rang out. The first sound since he had been in the room. The laughter came from his throne. Squinting in the darkness, he saw a man lying across his throne with his feet up.

"Whoever you are you will be whipped for your insolence," Herod shouted.

"King Herod, do you like what we've done with the place?" Tariq asked from the throne.

"We figured everyone here indulged themselves while you condemned our teacher to death." Drake's voice rang out from the area near the tigers.

The doors opened behind the king, letting in the morning light. The guard from the gate stood in the foyer grasping the three heads of Herod's servants by the hair. The light spilled in, and suddenly Herod could see all the people and animals around him were dead. Posed in seductive, macabre poses, all these people were dead. The guard took his scarf off of his face to reveal the clean-shaven profile of Peter. Peter tossed the heads at Herod.

Herod backed away from the heads, letting them smack on the marble floor. Peter propped the door open with the nude corpse of a nubile young woman. He began to advance on Herod. Herod turned around, realizing he was trapped. Drake closed in quickly and spoke to Herod.

"In addition to setting up the death of Jesus, guess what else we found you guilty of, King? We found groups of young boys caged in your bedchamber, boys that you use as sex slaves."

Tariq said, "We freed the boys to return to their families, so you might find yourself a bit short handed in the evenings."

Drake kicked the king's legs out from under him. The three men gathered around Herod staring down at him.

"What to do with a murderous pedophile who believes himself above the law?" Drake thought. No sooner had he thought it than Peter began walking to the throne. Tariq and Drake picked up on the thought. They lifted Herod to his feet. Peter climbed the steps and sat on the throne.

"Is this what it was like Herod? Passing down unjust condemnation on an innocent man from a position of power? Well you, sir, are not innocent. And I condemn you to torture and death!" Peter pointed angrily at him as he rendered his verdict.

"Castrate the monster!"

Herod fought with every fiber of his being upon hearing this. His arms held firmly behind him, he whipped his head back and forth, kicking to get free. Holding his arms with one hand the brothers ripped his tunic off of him. Herod managed to free his hand while Drake reached for his dagger. Herod punched Drake square in the mouth. Drake angrily ripped Herod from his brother's grasp and slammed him on the ground. Several of Herod's ribs broke and punctured his lung. He began wheezing and gasping for breath. Drake gripped his blade in one hand and Herod's member in the other and cut it off at the base. Herod didn't have the breath to scream. His mouth was gaped, attempting to suck any oxygen he could. Drake shoved the severed member in Herod's mouth and rolled him over on his face. Tariq looked at Peter on the throne. Peter now wearing Herod's crown, held a fist out with his thumb pointing down. Tariq jumped in the air as high as he could and came down knees first on the back of Herod's head. The sickening crack of Herod's head cracking echoed in the now silent throne room. Peter came down from the throne and dropped the crown on the nude, deceased body of the King. The men left the palace with two more stops.

Chapter 23

The men began to run, faster than they had ever been able to before, toward the place of the skull. Even with the stop to slay Herod, the men could easily overtake Judas. Judas had hurt his knee in a fishing incident and walked very slowly. In fact, had it not been for Jesus' insisting, they would have left Judas behind on several occasions.

They pushed ahead until they were at the top of the hill where Jesus' cross still stood. The oak cross stood soaked in wet blood still. They looked off in the distance at a lone tree. Beneath it Judas had wrapped a rope around his neck and fixed the other end of the rope to a branch. He was going to hang himself. The men sprinted toward the tree. As Judas stepped off the rock that supported him, he waited for the snapping of his neck. Instead he felt the arms of Peter catch him and hold him up. Drake jumped in the air and grabbed the rope, tearing it in half.

"You didn't think we'd let you off that easy did you?" Tariq asked.

Judas tried to wriggle out of Peter's grasp. Peter threw him to the ground and held him under foot while the men discussed what to do with him.

Judas couldn't believe what was happening. These men whom he had known for so long had come to exact revenge. He could hear them talking, but the noose around his neck had cut off much of his circulation, and he couldn't make out what they were saying. He felt himself being lifted off the ground and slung across Tariq's broad shoulders. The men ran for the nearby mountains where Jesus was entombed. They passed Jesus tomb and continued up the mountain. When they were halfway up the mountain, they stopped. He couldn't see what the other two were doing, but it was very loud. Tariq turned to make sure they were not being followed, and Judas saw that they were walking into a cave. The cave was pitch black with a stone slab in the back. The smell was putrid. It caused Judas to gag. Suddenly it dawned on him that they were in a tomb. By the smell of it, they were in a very old tomb. Tariq shucked Judas from his shoulders. Judas reached to loosen the noose, but Drake slapped his hands. Peter walked to the ancient corpse and grabbed several yards of fabric from the deceased. He walked back and bound Judas's hands behind his back. He then grabbed the remaining amount and bound his legs together. The noose was still choking him, causing his bloodshot eyes to bulge, but he had just enough air to keep from blacking out. They lifted him in the air and slammed him to the floor. Dust filled his compressed lungs. All three men slashed at their own skin causing blood to flow freely from their wrists. They forced it into Judas's mouth. The blood covered his face as it splattered from him mouth. He tried to fight it, but it was futile. The men watched Judas rolled on the floor crying.

"Please kill me," he screamed.

"No," Peter said. "You will live for eternity trapped in this hillside tomb with your own guilt until you go mad." He snickered as he saw Judas's eyes crystallize. "And then after you lose your mind, you will still be locked in here forever."

The men exited the tomb and worked together to push the massive stone back in front of the tomb. When the stone slammed back into place, they brushed off their tunics and headed for their last victim.

Chapter 24

Pilate was in his study waiting for Caesar to arrive. When he did, Pilate would have to parade him around the city. The infantry was assembled and ready to be reviewed. His wife was dressed in the finest silks of the Asian empire. And every servant in his jurisdiction had been made to bathe in the bathing pools. He even made sure that they didn't bathe with the Hebrew people. Pilate, however, was vexed. He could not concentrate on the crime figures in front of him. He could not help but feel like he had played an integral part in a murder. He would get up and wash his hands obsessively. He replayed the scenario in his mind a thousand times. How could he have acted differently without causing a riot? There seemed to be no answer. This city was filled with ignorant savages with no regard for the legal process. He dreamed of the day when he would be relieved from his post and sent back to the heart of Rome. Perhaps he could be a senator? He dried his hand for the fifth time and strolled out onto his balcony. He looked below to see his sizable army already amassing below. Tiberius Caesar was the second Caesar since his stepfather Augustus Caesar had died. He was a cruel and tyrannical leader. His sexual perversity was limitless. In fact, there was a good chance that he would spend a great deal of his time picking sexual conquests to take back with him to his home. If Pilate wasn't careful, Caesar might take his wife as well. He yelled for his runner. He heard the young boy running down the hall to the study.

"Yes, sir."

"Boy, let the guards at the bottom of the stairs know they can go outside and get into formation. I need to portray the largest force possible."

"Yes, sir … but who shall I get to protect you?"

"I will be fine. The entire eastern legion is outside my window. I have nothing to fear." The boy ran off to deliver the orders.

He walked to back into the study and closed the doors. He stood just inside the balcony and looked out. He could see the crosses in the distance used to crucify Jesus and the criminals. He closed the drapes so he wouldn't have to look at it anymore; besides, his trumpeter would announce the arrival of Caesar. He sat down and continued reviewing sanitation and crime numbers.

The three men ran the majority of the way to Pilate's compound. They stopped only to bathe in the river that ran along the road. After cleaning the blood from their arms and faces, they continued on their way. When they reached the entrance road to the manor, they observed the large gathering of soldiers and hid behind a brick wall on the perimeter of the compound. They followed the wall around to the backside of the house. They scaled the wall quickly and fell to the earth on the other side. They pressed themselves against the house and began slinking around to the side entrance. Peter put one finger to his lips as he came near the open door. He could hear soldiers inside. One soldier was talking about complimenting the other on the savage beating he gave the Jew yesterday. Peter could hear the voices of three guards laughing about stealing the now dead Jew's robes. They spoke of their irritation that they now had to work split shifts to cover the tomb since it was being rumored that his body would be stolen. And now on their day off they had to guard Pilate and stand in this lousy formation. Peter heard a fourth voice faintly telling the men to go get in formation. As the three guards exited the door, the three men grabbed them and cut their throats. They pulled the ceremonial armor and helmets off of the guards and put them on. They let themselves in the sparsely populated manor and headed up the stairs to the only room with the doors shut.

Pilate heard a light tapping at the door.

"Who is it?" he asked. There was no answer. Then, a moment later, there was another rap on the door.

"If you don't announce yourself, you may leave."

Pilate waited a moment more. When he thought the person had left, he heard another knock on his study door. He got up and walked to the doors, mildly irritated. When he opened the door, he saw three of his soldiers. They had mischievous grins and waited to be addressed.

"Well, what do you want?" Pilate asked in exasperation.

The men grabbed him by his throat. The one in the middle covered his mouth.

"Can you be quiet, Pilate?" Peter asked. "If you can, then we can talk; if you can't, then you die right now." Pilate nodded as best as he could, being held in the air by his throat. The men put him down.

"What do you want?" Pilate asked rubbing on his neck.

"We want to know how you plan on living with yourself after flogging and condemning an innocent man to the cross," Drake inquired.

Pilate stood up to his full six foot three inches. "You have no idea what it is like to govern this land. Do you think it is easy to control this horde of wild beasts? Do you think this is the first innocent man to be sentenced to death? I do what I must because if I don't, the Jewish Pharisees will lead a revolt, and I will lose my post and my head."

Drake replied, "I don't think those Hebrew Pharisees will be a problem to anyone anymore."

"Who are you people?" Pilate asked.

Tariq replied, "We are the Justice that people deserve. Not your brand of justice that can be bought or bartered for. We are the ones who will stand up to those who would see innocent men slain. We are here to claim your life for the murder of Jesus of Nazareth." Pilate turned away from the men and walked back to his bowl of rose water. He gazed woefully into the water. His reflection showed the age that this position has taken on him. The bags under his bright blue eyes and wrinkles at the corners of his eyes and mouth were evidence that public office was a death sentence. His reflection peered back him sullenly. He dipped his hands into the water and washed them again.

"I never wanted to have him killed. I tried everything I could to spare his life. If only he would have spoken in his defense, if he had said anything I could have used, I could have stayed his execution. It was as if … as if he wanted to die. He had come to grips with his fate and had embraced it. I washed my hands of his blood and, ashamedly I must confess, ordered his execution."

Drake grabbed his soaking forearm and spun him back around. "We are not here because of what you intended to do. We are here for what you did." Pilate pulled his arm free and composed himself.

"May I make a final request?" Pilate asked. "Please present my body in front of the troops. Tiberius Caesar is coming soon, and my death may speak volumes of the state of this province."

Tiberius Caesar was riding his chariot to the front of Pilate's compound. Normally he would ride horseback with a limited guard, but today he decided to unveil the new conscripts to Pilate and the eastern provinces. He rode with two thousand soldiers in tow. The men marched behind his chariot, the Roman banners waving in the front of the formation. Caesar thought to himself that whatever guard Pilate had presented would seem meager in comparison. He chuckled to himself as he rode through the main gates and saw the battalion of troops before him. A series of trumpet blows were sounded signaling his arrival. He rode through the break in the formations to the front. He wanted to see Pilate's face when he witnessed the new additions to the army, but alas, he was nowhere to be seen. Suddenly, a large object fell from the sky and landed in front of his chariot. He tugged the reins hard. He got off the chariot and walked around to see what had fallen. As he neared the front a look of horror came over his face; he was looking into the lifeless eyes of Pontius Pilate.

The three men had each put a hand around Pilate's throat and lifted him in the air. He didn't struggle as he had decided on dying a noble death. When the life left him Drake dragged him to the balcony and tossed his body over the edge on to the formation of soldiers below. He didn't let himself be seen, so the men could sneak back down the stairs and out of the back of the house. The men never saw Caesar or the Roman army below. As they got to the bottom of the stairs, Tariq grabbed Peter by the back of the tunic.

"Why don't we leave by the front exit?"

Peter replied, "We will have to face two or three hundred soldiers."

Tariq smiled, "We can't be killed, Peter. We can exact justice on all the guard that was present at Jesus' killing."

Peter looked at the ground. "We shouldn't press our luck, Tariq. We have gotten all the people responsible."

Drake pulled out two swords, twirling them in a circle. "These guys are responsible. We can take them, Peter."

Peter reached for his sword and slowly pulled it from its sheath. "If we are going to do this, then let us do this now while they're in formation and all their swords are sheathed and unsharpened. They have no shields while in formation."

The three men nodded in agreement and headed around the side courtyard to the front. As they turned the corner they were met with an entire army of soldiers, arms at the ready and shields intact, two hundred of the cavalry on horseback. They stared at over two thousand soldiers, who stared right back at them. There would be no retreat today as they heard Pilate's battalion of soldiers flanking them to the rear.

Caesar dismounted his white stallion and walked up the marble steps so that he could be seen by these three suspicious guards. All three men held their ground with no intention of running. Caesar eyed the men carefully. Caesar gave the order to have the men killed. Before the command had been fully materialized, the three men swung into action. The two brothers started swinging their swords with reckless abandon. Peter turned to the small army behind them and began attacking.

Caesar watched as seventy-five men were slain in a matter of minutes. The three men were being stabbed and wounded but seemed to heal and continued to fight. Caesar had seen this before, and a smile crept over his face in spite of his growing losses. Caesar yelled for the entire army to capture the men. Fifty more men were killed, but inevitably the three men were contained. He had their swords stripped from them and their hands bound together. He ordered their arms bound to their sides and their feet bound together. They looked like mummies when the process was done. The only things not bound were their heads. Caesar walked to the now bound men and approached Tariq. Tariq looked away disgustedly, and Caesar grabbed his jaw and forced his head up. He pushed back Tariq's top lip looking into his mouth.

"Interesting," Caesar exclaimed. He looked into Tariq's eyes for a moment. "Does this enrage you, boy?" He slapped Tariq in the mouth with the back of his hand. Tariq tried to free himself from his bondage with every fiber of his being. When he realized that he couldn't, he spit in Caesar's face. Caesar laughed at him and wiped his face off. "You will pay for that, boy," Caesar said.

"Bring them to the ship; tonight we sail to for Cyprus."

Chapter 25

The journey to the docks seemed to last only a few hours. The three captives, who had been on countless fishing vessels, had never seen anything that looked like this. It was polished oak from bow to stern. The sails were emblazoned with the royal Roman crest. A fleet of ships followed to carry Caesar's army. As the men were carried onto the ship, they were thrown into cages in the lower decks.

The three hadn't spoken a word. They communicated, however, through thought. The main idea of these thoughts was getting free. They could feel the boat begin to sway as it set underway. Within three hours, they arrived in Cyprus. What they should expect was anybody's guess. They were dragged off the boat and thrown over the backs of horses. The small procession headed into the mountains. Twenty soldiers and Tiberius Caesar led the way. As the terrain grew more treacherous, the horses were tied and left on the trail. The three captives were carried by the soldiers. When they neared the top, Caesar signaled for them to stop.

A large house amongst the overgrown foliage loomed or a cliff. They had arrived just in time. The sun was just dipping below the ocean. Caesar pulled the giant copper doorknocker. He slammed it three times against the door. A moment later an eye appeared through the small looking window. The door opened slowly. A stunningly handsome man opened the door. Although his skin was pale as the clouds, his wavy dark hair fell just below his shoulders. His chiseled jaw appeared to be made of stone, it was so sharp. He wore no tunic and revealed a flawless torso. No scars or imperfections to be seen. His mannerisms were far too graceful for any mortal man to have. But it was his eyes that caught the three captive's attention. They were as green as the Aegean. They were intensely bright, almost glowing against his white skin. Then he spoke, "To what do I owe his honor, Caesar?"

Caesar smiled widely as he gestured for the three captive men to be brought forward. "Greetings, Vladimir," Caesar exclaimed.

Vladimir looked at the men brought to his doorstep. The soldiers threw them down at his feet. Vladimir sighed and asked the soldiers if that was really necessary. Vladimir stepped back and invited Caesar into his home. Caesar warily took a step back and told him that would be unnecessary.

"I brought you a gift. These men are special. They committed heinous crimes, though, and I have condemned them."

"You have condemned them to what?"

"I have condemned them to you."

Caesar turned and walked back down the trail to his men. The three men remained lying at Vladimir's feet. He watched as the procession headed back down the mountain. He easily dragged the bound men into his home. He sat them on three wooden chairs and returned to the door to lock it. Next he walked over to the men and removed their gags. When he had finished, he pulled up a chair backwards and sat down on it, leaning his hands and chin over the backrest.

"So, what did you do to have the most powerful man in the world bring you to me?" Vladimir inquired. The men were perplexed as to why this man felt he had nothing to fear.

"We exacted revenge on those who would kill innocent men," Peter remarked.

"Uh huh," Vladimir replied. "Would it infuriate you to know that I have killed many innocent men and women?"

"It would only make me want to kill you that much more," Drake replied. "If I get free of this bondage, I promise you I will wipe that smug look off of your face."

Vladimir smiled. He stood up and moved his chair behind him. He kneeled down at Drake to look him in the eyes. He pushed Drake's mouth open and peered in. Drake couldn't resist him. Vladimir let him go and stood back up. He looked into the other's eyes as well.

"You aren't one of mine, but you are something special," Vladimir remarked.

"I will rip the skin from your face and feed your smiling lips to the creatures of the wild if it is the last thing I do," Drake threatened.

Vladimir walked to Drake and ripped the ropes around his shoulders apart with his bare hands. He watched as Drake freed himself and threw his chair out of the way so there was nothing separating the two of them. Tariq and Peter told him to free them so they would be sure to kill this thing, but Drake wasn't having it. He clenched his fists in rage and yelled as he rushed Vladimir. Vladimir stood his ground until the very last second and moved to avoid Drake's assault. Drake tried to turn around and face his opponent, but Vladimir was too fast. He grabbed Drake from behind and exposed a very sharp pair of fangs. His eyes turned to crystal, and he bit Drake. Drake struggled for a moment and then went limp. Vladimir dropped Drake's exsanguinated body to the floor. He stood over him for a moment catching his breath.

"I haven't tasted blood like that in centuries! You are from heaven? But you are not angels. I cannot pinpoint what you are. I suppose the only way to figure it out is another sample." He advanced on the other two men. After draining them both and leaving them still bound and draped over the chairs, he returned to the lone window overlooking the sea.

Three hours later, the men started show signs of life. Vladimir walked across the room to them. He used his fingernails to cut through the remaining men ropes on the two men. They were still dizzy and disoriented. The blood however had begun to pump through their veins again. Drake tried to push himself up from the floor but found he was still too weak to do it. He collapsed on the wooden floor. Peter began mumbling about how thirsty he was. When the men's eyes began to come back into focus they all felt the thirst burning through their bodies. Vladimir sat on the sofa across from the men sipping from a wine challis. Peter requested in a raspy voice for a sip of the wine. Vladimir grabbed the sack of wine and brought it to him. Peter began to gulp the wine, but found that it did nothing to quell the inferno raging inside him. Tariq ripped the sack from Peter and started chugging the wine. Again nothing happened to stop this insatiable thirst. They demanded water, as they weren't strong enough to get up themselves. Vladimir informed then that water would do nothing.

"Gentlemen, while you try to regain your strength, let me introduce myself. I am Vladimir. I am what you would call a vampire. More than that though, I am *the* vampire. I have existed over one thousand years. I am the oldest creature walking the earth. I take what life I need to survive. I am the descendant of one of the most royal families. My grandfather is the archangel Michael. My other grandfather is one you call Lucifer. I tell you this so that you understand that not just anybody has bested you. I am the only person, if that is what I am, who can explain what has happened to you. And more importantly, I will only spare your lives past this evening if you tell me what you are and how you came to be at my door."

Peter struggled to his feet. "I will tell you everything if you will spare our lives and tell us what is wrong with us."

Peter explained the series of events starting with their last supper. He explained the strange transformation that had occurred two days ago, and the vengeance they had bestowed upon their transgressors. Vladimir listened intently. Drake struggled to keep his eyes open, and Tariq sat perfectly still. He did not move, partly due to fear and weakness. Peter wrapped up the story as quickly as he could. He found that he was losing his voice, and he was losing his strength rapidly. Vladimir stood up. He paced in front of the weakened men. Stroking his short goatee, he walked out of the room. The men could hear voices in the other room. Vladimir strode back into the room with a young woman in tow. He was pulling her effortlessly by the elbow.

"I know of this man you speak of," he said. "I do not know him as a human, but long ago, when the earth was young, my parents told me of him. I only know you speak the truth because the blood that courses through your veins is royal blood. I have feasted on it many times. But not in many centuries have I had the pleasure." He looked longingly out of the window. The girl seemed to have given up any chance of escape.

"The angels and demons have long since been exiled from this planet. I do not know if the man that you speak of is truly the son of God, but I know that the blood in you is most certainly from heaven."

He thrust the girl before the seated men. He grabbed her wrist softly. He folded her hand over in his oh so gently. He grazed his thumbnail over the inside of her wrist. The scarlet blood began to flow from her wrist. She let out a shallow gasp. He then proceeded to do the same to her other wrist.

Peter was appalled. Drake, whose eyes were still closed, suddenly became extraordinarily alert. His eyes sprang open, and he could smell the elixir of life pumping out of her body. Vladimir held the girl's blood-soaked wrist out for Drake. He dragged himself out of the seat and took the hand. He began lapping at the girl's wrist. Tariq suddenly jumped up. He had caught the scent as well. It seemed taboo and shocking, but quite natural at the same time. He grabbed the other arm and began sucking on it. Peter was the last to pick up the scent. When he did, he wanted to push his friends out of the way. Vladimir, using his thumbnail again, cut the girls neck below the ear. Peter stepped between her outstretched arms and began drinking from the fountain of her jugular. As they drank, they could feel the life running through them. Their energy returned in a matter of moments. Within seconds they were becoming consumed with the blood. They drank harder and harder. The blood could not pump fast enough through the small cuts.

Peter could feel his mouth begin to throb. He pulled his head way from the girl for a moment and felt his fangs descend. His face had begun to rage. He sunk his teeth into the girl's throat, and the blood gushed out like a geyser. Seeing this, both Tariq and Drake pulled away. They watched as Peter held the girl in his grip. The blood began to call to the men again. They each began to rage and sank there new fangs into the girl's wrists. The girl began to shake violently as she went into shock. Had Peter not been holding her up, she would have slumped to the ground. As her heartbeat got softer, Peter started lowering her to the floor. When she took her last breath, the men all released her and pulled off instinctively. They stood up and started at the limp body of the girl. They had killed more men than they could count in the last two days, but this was the first innocent person they had killed.

This did not bode well, thought Peter. He felt an immediate disgust with himself. He could not deny, though, that he felt more powerful than he ever had.

Vladimir smiled at the men and beckoned them down the hall. The stunned men followed him through the house. He led them to a granite door in the back of the house. The door was solid and lacked a doorknob or handle. Vladimir pushed the door with incredible strength, and it opened slowly under the pressure he applied. When the men walked through, they found themselves standing in the dark. Vladimir grabbed a torch from the wall and with nothing more than a thought set the end of the torch ablaze. The illumination showed that they were on the cusp of a spiraling stone staircase. There were no handrails, and the light of the torch was there guide. Vladimir led them down hundreds of feet until they reached the base of the stairs.

Once there, they were greeted with the sounds of fearsome growling and chains clinking. The men found that they could see into shadows. As they took a step toward the door, they were confronted by enormous creatures. These drooling creatures were baring there fangs. Drake let his eyes scan upward into the snarling face of an eight-foot werewolf. Vladimir put his hand up, and the three wolves retreated into the shadows.

Vladimir led the men further into the darkness. Eventually he passed through an arch into a room filled with books. The walls were lined with thousands of books. The stone floor echoed beneath their feet. This unique room was a complete circle. It was then that Peter realized they were at the bottom of a dry well. The top of the well had been triple sealed.

Vladimir placed the torch in a torch sheath along the wall. The room was still quite dark. Tariq was squinting into the room. Vladimir realized the men's new vampire eyes were not completely sharp yet and with the power of his mind lit every torch in the room. With the bright light, they could see that there was an altar set up in the center of the room. The book that lay open was obviously the crown jewel of the room. The men walked to it. Vladimir had the men sit along the stone wall and began reading to them.

This was a book that he had been the primary author of. It was the history of the world, supernatural and otherwise. He read into the night. The men listened, hanging on every word. When he had finished, he had the men expose their necks. He bit them all. Holding the blood in his mouth he opened the book. He let the blood flow onto the page. It did not stain the page. Instead the blood seemed to be absorbed into the pages of the book. It quickly faded and disappeared.

Vladimir finally spoke, "You are truly special. You have the blood of the son of God, and the blood of the grandson of Lucifer in you. I now have your essence kept forever within these pages. Your power will be linked with mine and all others in the book for all time."

Drake asked, "Then what happens if the book is destroyed? Will we lose our power?"

Vladimir responded, "Possibly, but nothing has happened to the book in a millennium. Perhaps you didn't notice, but I keep a very close guard of my book."

"Still, how can we ensure its safety?" Drake asked.

"Your blood calls to the book now, and you will always know where it is. Come now, I will send you back into the world with the knowledge of what you are."

They ascended the stairs and headed back into the house. Vladimir led them out of the front door. "You must hurry if you wish to catch the midnight ferry back to the mainland. Travel only at night. The sun will burn your skin. Too much sun will kill you. Feed when you must. Do not reveal what you are. Gentlemen, do not make the mistake of feeling invincible. You can be killed. There are those chosen by God who wield powers you would never imagine. We are the most powerful supernatural creatures in

existence, but there are others who are quite powerful. My protectors, for example, are extraordinarily
strong and may be able to kill you.

"You must travel with your preternatural speed if
you wish to see your teacher. If this Christ is truly the
son of God, then the scripture says he will rise on the
third day. I wish you luck."

Chapter 26

The men watched as Vladimir shut the door.

"What the hell is preternatural speed?" Peter asked.

"I have a pretty good idea of what it is," Tariq replied.

"We have less than a day to travel back to Jerusalem, so I suggest we get moving," Drake stated.

The men began running shoeless down the mountain. They were picking up speed at an alarming rate. It took mere minutes for them to reach the bottom of the mountain. Within five minutes, they had reached the coast. The ferry had already left and reached the other side of the sea. Without the option of a ferry, they had to swim the full breath of the sea. It was over twelve miles across the dark water to the other side. The men jumped in fully clothed and began swimming. It took less than seven minutes before the men felt their stroke hit the shallow, muddy bottom of the shore. They began running in the direction of Israel, using the stars to guide them.

With two hours until dawn, the guards in front of Jesus' tomb were startled awake as the giant stone blocking the entrance was split in two. The guards were rendered unconscious by the blast. A figure immerged from the dark of the tomb and walked off into the night.

With less than thirty minutes remaining until sunrise, the three men realized they were not going to make it. They were in the middle of the Gaza desert, and there was no place for them to hide from the onslaught of the rising sun. Drake cursed and began running as fast as his legs would allow him to run. Tariq yelled after him for him to stop, but he kept pressing on. Suddenly his legs were knocked out from under him, and he slid face first over a hundred feet before coming to a stop.

Peter helped him to his feet, apologizing for knocking him down. Tariq had an idea to keep them all from burning. Drake and Peter watched Tariq dig up the earth with his bare hands with incredible speed. Within moments they understood and joined him in digging the massive hole. When it was dug they jumped in turned around and began pulling the loose dirt back into the hole, burying themselves until not a piece of clothing was uncovered. Just as they finished, the sun broke over the horizon.

When the sun had set again, the men uncovered themselves and pressed on. Peter still found it amazing that he no longer needed to breathe. He still did it because he was used to it, but holding his breath required no effort.

As they reached the house where the disciples were hiding, they saw that the door was ajar. The men were arguing with Mary. She was exclaiming how she had seen Jesus alive. The men did not believe her, and several of them were getting angry and calling her a liar. When the door burst open, Peter was in front. The silence in the room was deafening. Everyone stared at the three apostles. It was evident that they had undergone a major change. Aside from being filthy and covered in dirt, they appeared bigger and stronger. Their eyes were mesmerizing, and their skin was flawless.

"What has happened, Mary?" Peter asked.

"I saw Jesus today in the garden outside the tomb," she replied.

The disciples started to grumble.

"Shut your mouths, cowards," Drake yelled. "We have not forgotten that you group of tax collectors and cheats are also the cowards who let him be taken in the first place."

James stood up, "Who are you to judge us? You were busy sleeping when this occurred. How do we know you weren't in on Judas Iscariot's plan?"

Tariq flashed across the room at James. He grabbed him by the throat and lifted him straight into the air. He had already raged before he touched Simon. The disciples in the room shrank back at the sight of Tariq's fearsome face.

Suddenly, the air in the room began to shimmer. Tariq sensed it immediately and dropped Simon back to the earth. As the shimmering continued, the doors slammed shut, and the figure of a man began to form in the center of the room. When the shimmering stopped, Jesus stood before them. The disciples surrounded Jesus. The three apostles simply stared at Jesus from the corners of the room.

Jesus looked back at each of them with an accusing stare. After showing himself to his disciples Jesus told them to stay there as he walked outside with the three vampiric apostles. They walked out away from town under the moonlight.

"I know what you have done. I cannot say I condone it. I understand the sadness that you felt, but when have I ever advocated killing? You do not kill in my name. I had a plan, my friends. But you have undermined it. Now I must return to my father, and you three, my most beloved, must remain here forever. Vampires are not welcome in heaven. Their realm is here on earth. Perhaps if you die I can arrange for your entry, but I have died for the sins of man, not for the sins of vampires. I cannot promise anything. Perhaps if you prove yourself in my father's eyes and continue my church here, it will go a long way."

Peter nodded his head and stared at the ground. Jesus lifted Peter's chin so he was looking in his eyes.

"You will still be the rock and foundation of my church, Peter. But you are no longer the Peter I have grown to love. Once you have established the church, you will be martyred. Once they have buried you, rise at night under the cover of darkness. Once you have, you must ride to the land east of here. You must change your name. I recommend something from that region, perhaps Kristoff. I have always liked that name. Tariq, you and Drake must not harbor hate and vengeance in your heart. Your killings must stop."

Tariq began to sob. He spoke through the tears. "We have been like brothers since childhood. I have always been here for you. Not for your church or your disciples. I will only kill to survive, but I cannot promise you anything more."

Jesus looked at Drake. Drake looked at his brother, then back at Jesus. He was utterly vexed.

"My Lord, I don't understand. We did this for you. These heathens murdered you, and we did what was right. Your teachings be damned. Those men got what they deserved. I will not apologize. I stood by you and loved you. I gave you years of my life, and now, after all of this, you reprimand me!"

Drake stormed off into the darkness. Tariq kissed Jesus on the lips. His blood tears streamed onto Jesus. Then he turned and with a deep sigh walked in the opposite direction of his brother into the darkness. Peter agreed to do what Jesus wanted.

Several years later after Jesus had returned to heaven and the church had been founded, Peter was crucified upside down and martyred. One thousand years later in Russia, Kristoff could still feel the pressure of Jesus' hand against his chin, and the nails being driven through his own hands.

Chapter 27

Jayden stood in the middle of the living room. He had been holding his wife's shoulders and now walked over to hold Katie.

Aaliyah spoke first. "You are *the* Peter? As in the first pope, Peter?"

"Not in many centuries have I gone by that name. But yes, I was once upon a time known as Peter."

Jayden interrupted his wife's next question. "Your story is incredible, but I must push forward. How do I turn my beautiful daughter Katie into ... one of us? That Vladimir guy only bit you, you said. You didn't have to drink his blood. Can I do that with Katie?"

"Unfortunately, no, she must taste your blood. Vladimir was special. He was the first natural vampire."

"Oh my God," Jayden exclaimed. "You mean Vladimir became Vlad the Impaler? Who later became known as ... Dracula?"

"Your history and listening skills are impeccable. Indeed, he is the very one who turned me through venom alone."

Jayden sat stunned for a moment.

In the midst the discussion, Aaliyah felt her eyes drift toward the mantle over the fireplace. The images of Jenny and Brian staring back her made her soul drop. Brian was in his jiujitsu gi smiling as he received his first national gold medal. She remembered how her eyes swelled with tears of pride that day. Now her eyes swelled with red tears at the thought that she would never see him smile again. She wiped her eyes and tried not to look at Jenny's picture, but the pain was too much. Her baby girl was dressed in a satin red dress with shiny black shoes and white stockings. She was sitting on Santa's lap at a Christmas party. She had no idea that Santa was actually Ronin dressed to look the part. Jenny smiled from ear to ear. Her bouncing curls and eternally sweet disposition made her a favorite of everyone at the party.

Aaliyah remembered how Jenny had gotten ill after the party, and they took her home to take care of her. She could still feel the heat from her little girl's feverish skin. She could still recall running her fingernail through Jenny's hair while she slept with her head in Aaliyah's lap. She almost smiled, remembering later that night when Jenny was sleeping on Jayden's chest, and she threw up her Christmas cookies all over his chest and face. Jayden didn't freak out on the outside, but she could tell he wanted to throw up himself. Aaliyah picked her up and cleaned her off in the shower, brushed her teeth, and put her back in bed with them after Jayden changed the sheets and bedding. She silently wept at the memory.

Jayden said, "This is all so much to take in. What I don't understand is why me? Is this completely random? Would this have happened to anyone who purchased the book?"

Kristoff stood up and walked closer to the fire.

"Jayden, have you ever wonder why the occult has had such a scholastic pull over you? Have you noticed that you recover from injuries quicker than most? Have you at least considered your fortune that your children are … or rather were beautiful and physically gifted?" Kristoff turned to face Jayden.

"I have had my eye on you for a long time. Ten years ago while in Russia, Vladimir contacted me. I journeyed to his home, my first return trip since I was turned. I wondered why my wayward master would call on me after so many centuries. When I arrived, he was extremely vexed. He invited me in and led me down the stairs back to the library. As we approached the door, the Werewolves stood guard. They whimpered at the sight of Vladimir. Vladimir struck the biggest wolf in the face, sending it flying against the wall, its heavy chains bouncing on the stone floor. He cursed them for their incompetence. He opened the doors and led me inside. The stand where the book had once rested was empty, and light shone through the opening of the well above."

"I can still smell that son of a bitch Drake," Vladimir screamed.

Kristoff looked up to see the hole that Drake must have dug from the top of the well in order to freefall to the bottom.

"I need my book back," Vladimir said, a little more controlled.

"What does that have to do with me?" Kristoff asked.

"I created you both, therefore you owe me. You cannot refuse my order. It is an effect of the transformation. It is true of any vampires you make as well. I need you to get my book back."

"Even if I wanted to, where do I begin to look? I haven't see Drake in centuries."

"Your blood is in the book; it calls to you. You simply need to listen."

"But isn't your blood in it as well? Why don't you get it yourself?"

"First, I don't need to explain myself to you; you will do what you are commanded. But I suppose telling you would be the civil thing to do." Vladimir led him upstairs and out of the well. They walked into the main living quarters. Vladimir stood with his back to a blank sheet rocked wall.

"I have been working on a spell for some time, two millennium to be specific. My power has grown over the ages, and magic is no longer out of the question for me. The one thing I desire is to find my grandfather, the angel Michael. I want to stand before him in all his gallantry. I want to breathe in his essence. I want to look into his deep, passionate eyes. Then I want to rip his head from his shoulders. My reasons are my own, so do not bother asking why I would want such a thing. Call it daddy issues.

"Anyhow, I digress. In order to pull off this spell, I need my book first and foremost. And I need to find a living descendant of mine. I have poured tirelessly through the internet, and do you know what I found? Nothing. Not one person shares my likeness. So, I devised a method a tad more, shall we say, traditional. I brought in a shaman."

Vladimir bit his wrist and smeared it on the wall. The droplets began to fall and then miraculously rise and run across the wall, leaving a bloody trail in their wake. The blood began to take shape on the wall as a map of the earth. Las Vegas, Nevada began to fill in with blood and began dripping until a steady waterfall of blood appeared to be pouring from the wall.

"This city holds the last people of my bloodline. If you can find some way to get them in the vicinity of the book or even show an image of the book to him or her, they should be attracted to it, so much so that they would part with much to have it. I cannot go myself, as it would put me on the radar in heaven. I do a good job of staying beneath it here on my mountain. Michael knows that the incantation that would bring him to me would involve me leaving my home here on the mountain. If I send you, then he is none the wiser. Bring me my book and one of my heirs. I wish you luck, and if you get the opportunity, feel free to kill Drake."

Kristoff continued, "After this encounter, I began looking for, or rather listening for the book. I came

across it at a bank in Los Angeles California. Drake
had put it in a safe deposit box. I simply hypnotized
the woman working behind the counter, and when
she took me back to the deposit box room, I ripped
open the box and walked out with it. Drake has
hunted me diligently since then. He didn't know it
was I who stole it. He simply listens for the blood
calling him from the book.

"My next obstacle was finding a way for you to
see the book. It wasn't until I was hunting outside
an internet café that I got the idea from some of
my victims. So I posted it on eBay, which is seen by
more than ten million people a day. It was only a
matter of time until you and ten others contacted
me about the book. I persuaded one of my would be
victims at the internet café to find your IP addresses,
and subsequently your physical address, and I paid
you all visits. The others were slovenly, and I had a
hard time picturing them as Vladimir's descendents.
When I saw you, though, I knew immediately that
you were part of the bloodline. I mean your skin is
darker and hair is shorter, but there is no question
that the resemblance is there. When I offered you
the opportunity to buy the book for five thousand
dollars and you accepted, I knew you were the right
one. So one thing led to another, and now here we
are about to transform the last remaining mortal in
the bloodline into an immortal like her infamous
forefather."

"Wow, so what do I do to begin the transformation?" Jayden asked.

Kristoff walked over to Katie and Jayden. First, take her in your arms. Hold her tightly, as she may convulse at first. The drinking of blood is not natural at all, so if she has reservations about it, you should drain her so that an intense thirst sets in. When her heart beats so soft that only your supernatural ears can hear it, you must begin to feed her from yourself. I recommend biting your wrist. The blood flows freely, plus your fangs can pierce your own skin. After she has consumed the blood, she will begin to go through the same transformations that you did. A note of caution, though, beware that you don't give the blood too soon or too late. Either way can be lethal."

Jayden nodded in understanding and took his daughter into his arms. Katie was shaking, but smiling.

"Are you sure this is what you want, honey?"

Katie gripped her father's shoulder in affirmation.

Jayden let his fangs descend and bit his daughter as softly as he could. She still let out a mild yelp. The blood rushed into him swiftly. He could feel her vibrant spirit in the blood. However, his only concern was concentrating on the sound of Katie's heart. Katie began to swoon. She could feel the room spinning around her. Her father's granite hands were the only things holding her up. She felt the pressure on her throat cease, but the room kept spinning. She began to go into shock. All she could think about was how thirsty she was. She then felt moisture on her lips. It was warm, yet it cooled her parched lips.

With her eyes closed, she instinctively put her lips to the gushing liquid. She sucked harder and harder, forcing the liquid into her. As she reached to put her hands around the geyser, it yanked away forcefully. Her father's arms were no longer around her. She almost fell to the ground. Just before she hit her head on the ground, another set of arms were around her. The thirst was still consuming her, and she clawed at the air for more blood. Finally, another wave of liquid was at her disposal. She grabbed the arm and began to take long pulls of blood from the waiting arm. She felt the familiar feeling of fingernails being run through her hair. She ran her own fingers up and down the arms of her mother. When she was done, she began to convulse violently in her mother's arms. Aaliyah held her close and kept her head from whipping back and forth. Jayden, still woozy from being drained so quickly, struggled to get to his feet. Katie finally stopped thrashing.

When she finally opened her crystal eyes, her mane of curly hair was a mess covering her vision. Her mother swept the hair out of her eyes and smiled at her daughter the same way she did when Katie was first born. Katie got to her feet and walked slowly to her father. She felt like she was seeing him for the first time. He looked so much more impressive through her vampire eyes. She ran her hand along his jaw and saw every muscle in his face. She glanced down at his forearm and took his wrist. The wound had already healed. She turned back to her mother without saying anything and kissed her on the cheek. The room was still silent except for the hum of the refrigerator.

Her mother led her to the hall mirror. She covered her mouth as she looked at the stranger in the mirror. Every imperfection and blemish had dissolved from her skin. Her hair, which she spent so much time to make manageable, was a mane of soft, curly, golden tresses. She seemed to have lost her tan, but still she felt like she was glowing. The reflection was off somehow, though, as if the lighting in the room was not enough. She looked at Kristoff, who informed her that she would lose her reflection over time. It would take centuries, but it would happen. She looked back in the mirror. She lifted her shirt above her naval. Her stomach was always pretty flat, but now she could see a shadow of her abdominal muscles. Her belly button ring shined against her pale skin. She had never been a very busty girl, but she had to reach under her shirt and unclip her bra as it was now constricting her. Katie smiled from ear to ear and ran to her father jumping into his arms. Jayden laughed and held his daughter tight.

Now at door there was loud banging. The family looked at each other. Jayden released Katie and went to door looking out the peephole. He unlocked the door and opened the door. James rushed into the door. His face was flushed and he had a note in his hand.

"My dad's been kidnapped!" he exclaimed.

Chapter 28

Ronin awoke in a brightly lit well furnished living room. He was dizzy and discombobulated. He tried to remember what had happened last. He was in his own house, and James came home upset. He tried talking to him to no avail. He spent the day running errands and came home when the sun went down. He was walking up the driveway and … he never remembered getting to the front door. He looked around the room, trying figure out where he was. It was definitely an expensive hotel. His head was pounding, and his back hurt. He barely had the strength to stand up. He reached up to rub his sore muscles. His hand rubbed a pair of gashes in his neck. He could hear a pair of voices speaking outside his door. The door opened slowly, and a woman walked into the room. She paid no attention to him and was still carrying on her conversation with the person outside of the door.

"This is bullshit, Alexis. Drake told both of us to stay here with the human," Natalie said.

"No, Drake told us to take him. He said nothing about me staying here. Besides this hotel room is swanky." Alexis smiled an evil grin.

"You're such a bitch." Natalie sulked.

"Have fun, and don't you dare kill him until you are given the word."

Alexis exited the hotel room quickly, leaving Ronin and Natalie alone.

Natalie grabbed the television remote and jumped on the bed where Ronin sat unable to attempt an escape.

"What do you mean your dad's been kidnapped?" Jayden asked. "Kidnapped by whom? When did it happen?"

James thrust the letter into Jayden's hand. It was addressed to Jayden. Jayden read the handwritten letter twice and then handed it to Kristoff.

Peter,

I wish I could say it was nice to see you the other night. You have a great deal of nerve coming between the book and me. I stole it from Vladimir ... that makes it mine. That old fool tried to keep its secrets for himself. Now they are mine.

Unfortunately, I didn't safeguard it as well as I should have, and someone stole it from me. (I'm fairly confident it was you.) You tried to sell it to the philistine who you now protect. My coven has been waiting for the right time to strike. Did you think we didn't know where you were hiding? Since you took it upon yourself to turn Jayden, we decided to strike where it hurts most. We've taken his confidant. This man's life is in your hands. We will kill him tomorrow night at midnight if I don't have the book back in my hands.

And just in case that's not incentive enough, Tariq is returning to lead the coven with me. We both know you are no match for the both of us. Oh, and if you try to bring your fledgling with you, I will finish the job I started on his family. I will wait for you in front of the Bellagio Hotel on the Las Vegas strip. Meet me in front of the lake at 11:30 p.m. Don't try anything because remember, there are two of you and four of us. Hmm, seems kind of appropriate, I will get the book back on Halloween night. It's the same night that we were turned two thousand years ago.

Sincerely,
Drake

Kristoff crumpled the letter in his fist.

James inquired in an angry voice, "Are you Peter?"

Kristoff was lost in his thoughts. He didn't acknowledge James.

James got angry at being blown off. "This is your fault isn't it? Hey, you piece of shit, I'm talking to you," James yelled.

Kristoff was getting angrier by the second. He still wasn't paying any attention to James. The thought of Drake getting Tariq to help kill him was infuriating. James stormed toward him. He was seeing red and couldn't care less about anyone in the room at that moment. James cocked his extra large fist back and threw an overhand right at Kristoff just as Kristoff began to rage.

His fangs descended inadvertently into James's fist. James felt his hand break and the piercing of the fangs into his bone. His hand was stuck against Kristoff's mouth. He yanked and ripped the flesh of his hand wide open. His blood was flowing all over his arm as he held his hand next to his face. All the Endsley vampires stared at the bloodied arm and poised to attack.

Jayden was fighting with every bit of his being to keep from lunging. He yelled for James to get the hell out of there. James took off out the open door and headed toward his dad's truck. Aaliyah instinctively gave chase. Kristoff reached for a bowling bag on the floor and hurled it, complete with sixteen-pound bowling ball, at Aaliyah's head. It knocked her to the floor. She was up again in seconds, but Kristoff and Jayden grabbed her and pulled her upstairs where the smell of blood wasn't so strong. No one remembered that Katie was still standing there watching this ordeal transpire.

James jumped in the driver's seat and fumbled in his pocket to find his keys. His hands, slick with blood, dropped the keys. He watched in horror as they slipped and fell between the seats. He stuck his good hand awkwardly down in between the seats. He felt the key ring touch the tip of his finger, but it was no use. He would have to get out of the truck to get the keys. When he looked up, he saw Katie staring back at him through the passenger side window. She looked truly possessed. She was hotter than he had ever seen her but under some spell. She took a deep breath through her nose and suddenly her face began to contort, and her eyes crystallized. She shattered the window with one fluid punch. She reached in and grabbed the 230-pound linebacker and pulled him out of the truck like he was a ragdoll. She tossed him to the ground, where he bounced off the grass, and before he could try to move, she had mounted him and sunk her teeth into him.

Chapter 29

Aaliyah was starting to return from the blood frenzy. She had retracted her fangs and was kneeling in the corner. Jayden heard the commotion on the lawn and looked out of his bedroom window to see his daughter murdering his godson. Jayden held his breath and jumped through the glass of the second floor window. Raging on the fly, he tackled his daughter.

James lay writhing in pain on the lawn while Jayden pinned his daughter to the ground. A security light turned on above the garage on the house across the street, and the nosey old woman came out to see what was going on. Holding Katie down with one arm, Jayden grabbed a stone and hurled it at the security light. The light shattered and cast the house back into darkness. The old woman thought that the bulb had fallen out and broken. She walked back into her house complaining of the poor job the electrician did on her house. Katie was fighting fiercely to get up and feed. Jayden was running out of time to save James. He flipped his daughter over and put her in a modified sleeper hold. He knew that oxygen was not a requisite for vampires, however if he put her in a blood choke she should black out. No blood to the brain equals passing out. And just as he thought, within seconds her body went limp.

He grabbed James and pulled him into his arms. Jayden looked at his wrist to draw blood, but his veins had shriveled. He hadn't fed tonight, and didn't have the strength. Plus he and Aaliyah had given Katie all they had. Perhaps Kristoff could do it, but he hadn't fed either. There was precious little time as James breaths were growing shallower. Jayden grabbed Katie and pulled her over to James. He bit her neck so that the rich blood would flow, and lowered her neck to James's mouth. James was beginning to convulse and wouldn't open his mouth. So Jayden manually opened his jaw and let the blood flow into James. Like the others, after a few drops James latched on like an infant and drank until Kristoff came to the window and told Jayden that was enough. Jayden pried his unconscious daughter away from James.

While James's body proceeded to die right there on the lawn, Jayden hopped the back wall and grabbed the yapping dog of his neighbor and snapped its neck. He brought the fresh carcass back over the wall into his own yard. He pulled the head off of the dog, and while the blood was not as alluring as a human's, it still held an appeal. He let some fall on Katie's lips, and then he drank some himself. Katie began to come to when the blood worked its way into her mouth. She opened her eyes to the sight of her father drinking from the headless corpse of a dog. She started to scream when a strong hand clamped over her mouth. She looked up to see the liquid pupils of James's vampire eyes.

Chapter 30

Blistering desert winds swirled around the airstrip in Baghdad. The door of the C-130 aircraft opened to reveal a dark, unfinished interior filled with soldiers. Many of them were holding their stomachs from the evasive maneuvers the pilots did while approaching the airfield. The dim red light was the only illumination until the desert sun blasted its way through the open door. The soldiers sat in makeshift seats comprised of cargo netting. Stephan often wondered why they travelled with all of their armor on. It was very heavy and made the twenty-six-hour flight unbearable. A rookie Lieutenant stood at the front of the plane. He started yelling for everyone to dismount the aircraft. One by one, the soldiers exited the plane. Many of the new soldiers were clutching their weapons tightly and looked for guidance from a superior. Stephan, however, was a seasoned vet. When all of the soldiers put in hearing protection to dim the sound of the roaring plane engines, Stephan put in his Mp3 player.

He walked brusquely toward the five-ton trucks parked outside of the airfield with everyone else. They packed the back of the massive pickup trucks with soldiers. It was nine a.m., and already the temperature had reached 127 degrees. Stephan put his military-issued Oakley sunglasses on and pulled a scarf around his mouth and nose to block the sun and the sand. Within minutes, they were headed to Camp Victory.

When the soldiers arrived, they dismounted the trucks and were in formation. They were standing in front of a bombed-out warehouse.

"Welcome to your new home for the next year, soldiers," Lieutenant Villarreal said.

Stephan rolled his eyes because he had lived here twice before. In fact he was on the detail responsible for cleaning the blood out of it when they first captured the installation. There were only two good things about this place. First, it had indoor plumbing. While the hot water went out at least three times a month it was better than nothing. More importantly, it had air conditioning. While it went out as frequently it was infinitely better than sleeping in tents. The soldiers went into the building and started setting up areas for them to live in within this large warehouse. It was filled with cheaply made bunk beds, the kind of beds that rocked if you leaned against them. The person on the bottom bunk was always in mortal terror of his bunkmate crashing down on him. Privacy was a huge issue. The leaders spilt the building into two areas: the north end for the males, and the south end for the females. The soldiers had two flimsy aluminum wall lockers apiece. These were strategically placed around a soldier's bunk. If done properly, you could hang your poncho from it and create a 6x6 room that you and your bunkmate would share for one year.

The rest of the day would be used to get accustomed to the installation. The high walls with razor wire and guard towers, and the fact that people wanted to kill you, made this place a prison of sorts. If it weren't for the gym and some good friends, a person could break out here.

The next day the platoon was told to report to Al Faw palace. This palace was used as a summer home for Saddam before the war. It was ordained with marble columns and massive chandeliers. Stephan had once leaned over the twisting stairwell and taken a piece of crystal of a chandelier only to find out it was made of plastic.

The platoon was supposed to meet up with the unit they were replacing to go on a mission. When they arrived, they were escorted into a dim room with folding chairs. Everyone was relatively quiet except for one soldier from the other unit who kept bragging aloud about all the A-rabs he had killed in the last year.

When they had sat for ten minutes, the door opened, and a young man walked in. He was dressed in civilian clothes and couldn't have been older than thirty. He began speaking to them while he was writing notes down on a pad of paper. Unlike all the other soldiers and civilian contractors, he wore slacks and a polo shirt. His shoes were completely out of place. The shine on them implied that he never wore them outdoors, and he never left the palace.

"Good morning, soldiers. I am Martin Harper, and I will be briefing you on today's objective." A projector suddenly turned on, and a man's picture and biography appeared on the board. "This is Hassan al Zahieri. He is the main financier of explosives in the Middle East. It has been impossible to track him down until now. Last week our intelligence shows that he made several trips to a small village outside of Baghdad. We were informed that he has two sick children that he went home to check on. Our sources say he will be there tonight, so we must strike while the iron's hot. Next slide please."

The slide changed and showed a satellite image of the small town.

"The objective's house is located here. There are no indications that any surrounding houses are hostile. This town is extremely old, and we do not want to upset the people. Having said that, we will not be conducting an air assault."

There were several groans in the room.

"We will move in by convoy at midnight. First platoon will cordon the area, and second platoon will move against the objective. This is a capture mission, gentlemen, not a kill mission."

More groans came from the room. Stephan leaned forward in his chair and raised his hand.

"Mr. Harper, what assets will we have available to us?"

"Aside from your rifles and machine guns, you will have unmanned aerial vehicles in the air watching you, as well as Apache gunships on stand-by. Don't forget most of the homes in this region don't have roofs, so we can see everything."

"Will the medivac team be ready in case someone gets shot?" Stephan asked. "Because the last time I was down here, the Air Force took their sweet time to get to us, and somebody died."

"Did you plan on getting shot this time around?" Mr. Harper asked smugly.

"Of course the Air Force will be on alert for this mission. If you play everything by the book, this snatch and grab should be seamless." Mr. Harper said.

Stephan raised his hand again and started speaking. "So were you planning on getting those shiny shoes dirty and going on this mission, sir?"

Mr. Harper laughed and said, "Eight years in the Air Force is as dirty as I plan on getting. These are Italian leather, Sergeant. I get paid the big bucks to think; you get paid to play in the mud."

Chapter 31

That night the soldiers took their final briefing of the small town and climbed into the military vehicles that would convoy to the destination. Being in the rear vehicle, Stephan had the misfortune of having a gunner standing in front of him the whole ride. He had been the gunner before and he did not miss it. Not only was it uncomfortable standing for such a long time, but when an IED exploded and the truck rolled, the gunner almost always died.

The convoy twisted and turned, following the desert terrain. They traveled through the deserted streets of Baghdad. The buildings were war torn and barely standing. Even the stray animals along the street had felt the pain of war, as they struggled to find scraps of food along the road. As they continued to drive to the outskirts of town, they arrived in the small village. They pulled just shy of the house, and Stephan's platoon began to cordon the area around the house.

The same ignorant jackass who had made the snide comments earlier led second platoon. The leader spoke into his headset, "This is Alpha team leader, Ford, and we are going in."

Stephan was kneeling down beside the neighboring house observing the night. He could hear the gunshot in the target house. He remained vigilant in case someone came to aid the terrorist leader. The house he was posted in front of had few sounds in it. He knew that several families would share one house. The door opened, and a little girl poked her head out to see the commotion. Stephan pointed his rifle at the ground, as to not frighten the girl. He held one finger over his lips to signal the girl to be quiet. She nodded her head and pulled the door closed. Stephan thought to himself, *A scarred child is the same in any language.* Suddenly, the target door burst open, and Alpha team was coming out with a corpse. An officer was yelling at Ford.

"This was a snatch and grab, not a kill mission. The man didn't offer any resistance. You damn dummy, you are looking at a court marshal."

Ford shoved past the lieutenant and headed toward Stephan's position. "We heard on the radio that there was activity at this house too."

Stephan looked incredulously at Ford. "There was a little girl who looked out of the door, big deal." Stephan said.

Ford pushed past Stephan shouting, "Then she was probably a look out for the terrorist, you idiot."

Stephan tried to grab Ford, but it was too late. He threw the door open and hit Stephan in the face with it. In the moment Stephan tried to shake the cobwebs from his head, he heard the weapons' fire ring out. He pulled open the door and saw the dead bodies in each room. Little girls and boys hanging on to their parents were bleeding from the head wounds sustained from Ford's merciless shots. Ford came over the radio, "First floor cleared, I'm moving upstairs."

Stephan ran toward the stairs and tackled the much larger Ford. Ford wrestled with Stephan for what seemed like an eternity. Stephan finally slammed Ford's hand against the floor until his rifle came free. Stephan slapped it out of Fords grasp.

Ford looked exasperated and shouted, "Fine I'm through." When Stephan started to get off of him, Ford pulled his switchblade and shoved it into the armor-free ribcage of Stephan. Stephan stumbled backward. He could taste the blood coming up his throat and into his mouth. He pulled the knife out and tried to call for a medical evacuation, but Ford ripped his headset off his head. At the top of the stairs, a man stood staring at the mêlée. Ford, feeling someone watching him, grabbed his pistol from his side and pointed it up the stairs into the darkness.

"Who's there?" he screamed.

He let his thumb slide over the flashlight button on his pistol and was staring into the raging face of Tariq. Tariq flashed down the stairs and grabbed Ford by the neck. Ford fired three shots into his attacker, but the bullets did nothing. Tariq shoved his hand into Ford's Kevlar armor and through his chest. He pulled Ford's still beating heart out of his chest cavity and bit into it. Then he kicked in both of Ford's knees, shattering the bone and breaking the joint so that he was kneeling backward at an inhuman angle. Tariq left him there in that position. He moved toward a hunched over Stephan.

Stephan saw what transpired, but was in too much pain to move from the wall that was supporting him. But as he saw Tariq's bare feet move toward him, he stood straight up. He wanted to look into the eyes of the man who would kill him. Tariq stood inches from Stephan's face. The two men stared at each other for over a minute. Tariq then cocked his head toward Stephan.

"You have a good soul, warrior. I wonder, though, do you have what it takes to bring justice to the wicked?" Stephan panted, unable to respond. Blood was pouring out of his side and his mouth. "You have only minutes until your heart stops beating."

Stephan fell to his knees, unable to stand any longer. His armor felt like the weight of the world was on his shoulders. Tariq put his hand on Stephan's face. Stephan, looking at the floor, didn't want to die, but felt death's icy grip slowly taking him from this world. Tariq plunged his fangs into Stephan momentarily and then slit his own wrist and offered it to Stephan. Stephan reluctantly took the blood into himself, as per Tariq's instructions. While Stephan's transformation took place, Tariq spoke, "We are now linked forever, master and fledgling. I have given you back life, and in return you will help me take the lives of those who would kill needlessly. Your time as a soldier has come to an end. I can hear your unit looking for you." Tariq grabbed Ford's fresh corpse and dragged it to the new vampire.

"Eat quickly, and we will be off. We have a long way to travel, and you are going to meet your new family."

As the tandem left, the unmanned aerial vehicle in the sky captured the entire episode.

Chapter 32

Now back in the house, James stood in the living room staring at the Endsleys. The family was standing shoulder to shoulder, with Kristoff in the back. Katie stepped forward and ran her hand over James's broad shoulders and down his massive chest. James stood perfectly still, not breathing. Katie looked up into his eyes and saw the liquid color of oak staring back at her. She saw the tiniest hint of fangs in his agape mouth. He was a roman statue. His stature was magnificent to behold. His hair was cropped tightly to his head. His biceps were the size of bowling balls, and his legs looked as though they belonged on a thoroughbred. James finally grabbed her hand from his chest and stepped backward.

"I'd have to be an idiot not to realize what has happened to me. I've seen enough vampire flicks to know what is going on. What I don't understand is how long have you been vampires?" James inquired.

Jayden responded, "I've only been a vampire since the night Brian and Jenny were murdered." Nodding in the direction of Katie. "She has only been a vampire minutes longer than you have."

Aaliyah interrupted the discussion, "Yes, and I have been a vampire for a few nights now, but we have other things to discuss. Your father has been kidnapped, remember?"

James's eyebrows furrowed, and he sat on the edge of the suede couch. The couch groaned beneath his considerable weight. Jayden stood before the other vampires in the room. The orange flames from the fire reflected in his eyes as he spoke. "We are going to get your father back, James, and this is how. This dark coven doesn't know that we are all vampires, so we have the element of surprise. They are much older, which means they are much stronger. So we will divide and conquer. We will dismantle them one by one. The first thing we need to figure out is where your father is."

Kristoff spoke up, "I might know how to find them." He grabbed the Book of Eternal Night and opened to a page that was fairly worn. He began to read the words softly, and his eyes began to glow.

Jayden read the title of the chapter over his shoulder: Incantations for finding vampires.

Kristoff began to think aloud. "They wouldn't leave Pagan or Alexis in charge of guarding a mortal. That is beneath them. Drake almost certainly won't be with him either. We need to find Natalie." He continued to read the incantation. Suddenly, he dropped the book and began looking around. It was as if he were no longer in the room. In fact he was now looking through Natalie's eyes. As she lolled around the room, she passed a window and saw the bright lights of a medieval castle across the street.

"I see a castle," Kristoff said. "It's across the street. Where am I?"

The group looked at each other perplexed. A knowing smile crossed James's face as he stood up and shouted, "You are looking at the Excalibur casino. So you must be in the MGM Grand."

The group ran to the MGM Grand as it was faster than driving. As they entered the lobby, Katie asked the obvious question, "How do we find her?"

"That part is easy," Kristoff said. He walked up to the bellhop and described Natalie to him. He was glamouring the bellhop, and he knew instantly who Kristoff described, as she was the most attractive woman he had ever seen. He told her that she was in a sky loft on the top floor.

Just to be sure, though, Kristoff took the elevator to the 15th floor and grew quiet as he began inhaling deeply. When he caught her scent, he reached and out hit the emergency stop, then returned to the first floor. He stepped out of the elevator, and the group walked back outside.

"She is up there," Kristoff said.

Jayden spoke up, "Then here's what we will do ... "

Natalie had been having her way with Ronin all evening. She had made both a slave and a meal out of him. She fed on him when she was hungry and forced him to do humiliating, degrading, and depraved sex acts for her amusement. He was begging her to kill him when she heard a light rap at the door. She shouted at the door that they were to be left alone. The knock happened again. She got up to answer it.

When she opened the door, no one was there. She began to shut the door when she picked up the faint smell of vampire. It was too new to be from Alexis earlier. She closed the door, knowing Ronin was too weak to try to escape. She followed the scent to the elevator. She waited impatiently for the elevator to get to her floor. She turned to face the hotel room down the hall, making sure Ronin didn't try anything. The elevator dinged, signaling its arrival. As the doors slid open, Natalie turned around to get in and found herself face to face with Aaliyah and Katie.

Her smile spread across her face from ear to ear. Her fangs descended, and she was elated with her good fortune. These idiots had come to find their friend. Ronin must have used the phone when she wasn't paying attention. Oh well, she couldn't believe her luck. She pushed the terrified girls back into the elevator. As the doors closed, and the elevator began its long descent, James came sprinting up the stairs and burst into the room.

His father lay covered in his own blood and handcuffed to the bed. He coughed up blood as he tried to shake the blindfold from around his eyes. His clothes were ripped, and his entire body was swollen from the abuse. James grabbed a clothing pin from the coffee table and covered his nose as not to go into a blood frenzy. James broke his dad's shackles and gently lifted him from the bed. Covering him with a sheet, he carried him down stairs and out the door, running for the hospital.

In the elevator, the girls stood shivering against the back of the wall. Aaliyah asked in a shaky voice, "What are you going to do to us?"

"The same thing we did to your little girl and pathetic son. I'm going to kill you," Natalie replied. She laughed a sadistic laugh. At that point Katie and Aaliyah stood up, looked at each other, nodded, and raged. The stunned Natalie couldn't move fast enough as the young vampires began savagely beating her. She slumped in to the corner of the elevator as the women rained down strikes from above. Aaliyah swung a devastating right hook and knocked out Natalie's fangs. Katie then kneed her in the face, shattering her jaw. Then the blood began flowing, and the girls dropped to their knees and began ripping the flesh from Natalie's body. Finally, when she was nothing more than a quilt of skin, the woman grabbed her head and ripped it off of her spine.

The elevator was coming to a stop, and Katie hit the top floor button to send it back up after it stopped for them. As the elevator dinged for the first floor, Jayden and Kristoff had large rolling laundry baskets, and the girls climbed in and covered themselves with towels. The door to the elevator closed, and carrying the headless corpse of Natalie, it began to climb back to the top.

As Ronin lay in the hospital intensive care unit, James excused himself and began to jog back to the meeting area in the Endsley house. As he stayed to the shadows of the streetlights, he stopped abruptly. Sitting at the stop sign were the two gangsters that tried to kill him twice before. Their black SUV had rap music pulsating at deafening volumes. A young man approached the vehicle and handed the men money in exchange for a white substance in a small baggie. James pulled the hood of his sweatshirt on and approached the driver. The driver lowered the window and leaned out, not recognizing James.

"Whatchu want, homie?"

James looked up and down the street. Seeing no law enforcement and only one other person walking in the other direction, he leaned into the driver to keep the transaction clandestine and suddenly sank his fangs deep into the driver's throat. This was not merely for food, but for savage revenge. He ripped at his throat, pulling out chunk after chunk of soft flesh. The passenger, in a panic, pulled out a handgun and aimed it from point blank range at James. James reached up and put his thumb over the end of the barrel. The gun fired and exploded in the passenger's hand. It took a good portion of his hand off. James pulled the driver's side door open and threw the driver to the floor in a crumpled dead heap. He climbed into the driver's seat and grabbed the passenger by the back of the neck. The gangster began pleading for his life, but James grabbed the young man's face and pulled the skin from his skull. Just before he died, he watched James slash the rest of his torso to ribbons.

Chapter 33

Stephan awoke in the darkness. He was not so much awake as aware. He could barely move and fought to open his eyes. As he forced his eyes open, he could feel the pressure of something trying to keep them closed. Once his eyelids were open, he was still blind. Panic began to set in. He couldn't remember where he was or what happened after he left with this man named Tariq. He opened his mouth to scream, and it immediately filled with soil. He was buried alive! As the terror set in he felt the earth tremble. An arm sliced through the dirt above him. The fingers wrapped under his armpit and dragged him to the surface. As the surface split around him, the moonlight baptized his filthy body.

He coughed the dirt out of him lungs and shook the dirt from his hair. He looked down to see Tariq kneeling down dusting off his hands. Tariq stood up and stretched his long limbs. He tilted his head toward the Euphrates River and told Stephan to follow him. The men disrobed and stepped into the water. During the day the river was filled with people washing clothes, bathing, and frolicking. In the middle of night it was still and silent.

The rippling of the water disturbed the sleeping water life. Stephan watched a frog jump into the water and swim away. The men washed the grime from their skin and hair. They scrubbed their clothes against the rocks in the riverbed. The silt from the clothes shimmered as it slowly descended in the water. They wrung out the clothes and laid them on the riverbank. The nude men swam back into the water, letting it stream past their faces under the surface.

As they treaded water, Tariq told Stephan of the centuries he has spent in the Middle East. He has fought in countless wars. Anytime the oppressed needed protection, he would fight on their behalf. Was it any wonder that Afghanistan had never been defeated? The Russian superpower was turned away. How did the Americans, with the greatest army the world had ever seen, have so much difficulty in an impoverished nation like Iraq? When southern Lebanon was destroyed by Israel, Tariq had gone to provide protection to many of the refugees. The patriotism in Stephan was conflicting with his new-found love for his vampire master.

"But you have killed many of my brother and sisters. I cannot condone that, Tariq."

"How many of my countrymen have you slain, Stephan?"

Stephan considered this for a moment. War had casualties on both sides. How do you justify your killings because you believe your people are more sacred, or your cause is more righteous? Tariq cupped the water and let it fall through his hands.

He addressed Stephan, "The point is there are warriors who fight to protect the weak, and those who kill for sport. You are a kindred spirit, Stephan."

"I never wanted to be a vampire," Stephan said with a solemn face.

"You never wanted to be betrayed and killed by your fellow soldier either," Tariq said.

The men swam for to the bank of the river. They put on their clothes and began walking toward the airport.

"So what's on our agenda?" Stephan asked.

"I must return to my brother in America and help him with an old adversary. He claims that our old enemy has begun slaying in cold blood. According to my brother, this vampire has gone mad with age and killed a small girl and her older brother in Las Vegas, Nevada. He kidnapped the father and brainwashed him. We don't know if he is still alive or if he has been killed. He must be stopped."

Stephan's jaw dropped. "That's my brother's family that was murdered." Stephan said. *My brother has been kidnapped?* he thought.

The men hypnotized the ticket agent and customs agent. They boarded the plane destined for the city of sin.

After they touched down, Tariq headed to the pay phone and called Drake. Drake informed them of the meeting tonight with Kristoff.

"Will we meet them tonight?" Stephan asked.

"Perhaps, if Drake needs us," Tariq replied. "We wait by the phone for the call."

Chapter 34

As the time drew closer to for the meeting Kristoff stood in front of the man-made lake of the Bellagio. Hundreds of costumed tourists walked past him. Some of the tourists were families looking at the lights of the city, while others were drunk to the point of intoxication, celebrating some life-changing event. Bachelor parties, divorce parties, twenty-first birthday parties, these people came in search of a once-in-a-lifetime experience. While others were there merely to celebrate Halloween in Sin City, Kristoff's mind was racing, and emotions filled his heart, yet his face remained stone. The water show began on the lake with classical music being pumped out of the speakers and jets of water being shot into the air. Kristoff watched as the water danced, bending back and forth in the air like Poseidon himself was controlling it. Suddenly he picked up the scent.

The citizen's area transit bus stopped on the strip, and Drake stepped off of it. He was unaccompanied and strode across the busy street toward Kristoff. Kristoff could smell the scent of more than one vampire. He let his eyes scan the tourists on the street. He could not find them. Drake approached Kristoff. The men had less than twelve inches between them. Drake smiled and leaned into hug Kristoff. Kristoff stepped back, avoiding contact with him.

"Come on, Peter, surely you harbor no hard feelings?"

Kristoff holding a book close to his chest, shot back, "We have no reason to embrace, as you have no heart left."

Drake looked down at the book in Kristoff's arm. "You don't think that I am fool enough to believe that you brought the book and came alone, do you? I can smell your fledgling"

Kristoff pulled the book from his chest and handed it to Drake. Drake looked at the cover and read the title, *The Holy Bible.*

"Is this a joke?"

"I think it might help you to remember the teachings of Jesus. He never wanted this slaughter fest through the ages."

Drake tossed the Bible into the lake.

"Here's the deal Peter. In my hand is a phone. The next call I make will be to Natalie. She will then snatch the life from your fledgling's companion."

Kristoff had anticipated this. "Then make the call, because I have no intention of parting with the book," Kristoff said.

Drake stared at Kristoff for a moment, "Very well then."

Drake scrolled through his directory, and when he landed on Natalie, he pressed talk.

Kristoff looked past Drake over his shoulder as though he was signaling Jayden.

Drake caught the glance and quickly turned around. Kristoff quickly grabbed the phone from Drake's hand and grabbed him into a choke hold. Leaning against the railing, Kristoff ended the call with his thumb and pocketed the phone. Drake elbowed Kristoff in the stomach, loosening his grip. Kristoff kicked Drake in the back, sending him flying onto Las Vegas Blvd. Drake was hit immediately by an oncoming pickup truck. Drake's flailing body smashed the front end of the truck and caused a small pile up.

Drake pushed himself off of the pavement and turned back to Kristoff, who stood on the edge of the lake. Drake raged, lowering his fangs and racing toward Kristoff, who didn't move. Drake suddenly stopped in his tracks as Jayden sprung from under the water and leapt over Kristoff. Fangs bared and raging himself, he descended on Drake. Crashing to the ground, he landed on top of Drake, landing punch after punch.

Kristoff fled with the phone. Drake's strength allowed him to finally kick Jayden off of him. The two men stood toe to toe. Blood covered Drake's face and Jayden's fists. As the men circled each other, Drake's wounds began to heal. He suddenly began to laugh and stopped. Pagan suddenly appeared behind Jayden. He had been down the street just out of eyesight. Jayden tried to put both men in front of him but realized it was futile. He let out a vampire roar that caused car windows to shatter.

"Kristoff left you to die, fledgling. Now we will finish the job we started the night we killed your family."

Just then a bright blue Lamborghini came screaming down the street. As it neared the three men, the driver threw on the emergency brake and began to power slide. As it spun, the passenger side door opened, and James sprang from the seat and launched himself at Pagan. Pagan, not expecting this, was tackled over the railing and into the lake. The driver hopped out of the car and raced around to Drake. Aaliyah, with the rage of a mother who lost her children, hit him with everything she had. Drake went reeling over the edge. James climbed out of the water with his arm dislocated. As he was almost out, a monstrous hand reached out of the water pulling him back in.

"Hey, blood bag!" a voice screamed from behind Aaliyah. She turned around to see Alexis running from across the street. She had been in the lobby of the adjacent hotel. Drake had instructed her to stay out of sight. But she couldn't let her mate be ambushed without helping him.

"I've got this bitch under control," Aaliyah said. She ran to meet Alexis in the street. Alexis speared Aaliyah, driving her head back into the pavement. Alexis was far stronger than Aaliyah, but Aaliyah was a much better fighter having trained jiujistsu with her husband and kids for several years.

Aaliyah blocked her face from the blows being dropped from above. From her knees, Alexis was wildly throwing punches. Aaliyah's legs were wrapped around Alexis, keeping her from mounting Aaliyah's chest. Aaliyah suddenly remembered what her husband had said in the last match she lost. This was a similar fight with a larger and stronger opponent. As Alexis threw another loop-ing punch, Aaliyah caught her arm and wrapped her legs around Alexis's throat. Alexis fought to free her arm to no avail. The triangle choke being applied stopped both blood and oxygen from reach-ing Alexis's brain. Aaliyah kept the pressure applied after the thrashing stopped, and Alexis went limp. Aaliyah's eyes began brimming with bloody tears as she saw the heart-shaped locket hanging around Alexis's throat. It was the locket she had given Jenny. Keeping her legs in place, she ripped off the locket. Then she twisted her thighs as hard as she could, snapping Alexis's neck. Then digging her nails into Alexis's tough vampire skin, she broke her spine with both hands and pulled her head off.

Chapter 35

The pay phone rang twice, and Tariq answered.

"Brother?"

"Once upon a time we were," Kristoff responded.

"Peter?

"So it's true, you did come back to kill me?"

"You deserve it, old friend."

"Well your coven is in the process of dying. You should have known that turning your back on the teachings would have consequences." Kristoff responded.

"Where is Drake?"

"From where I am watching, he is being beaten by my fledgling."

"You know I cannot let you live if you allow my brother to be killed."

"You mean the way the apostles let our master be killed? No, I will take part in his death if you don't promise to return to your misguided war on Christianity."

"My war is against evil. Not against Christ. And now it's against you, old friend."

Tariq hung up, and he and Stephan began running toward the Bellagio.

The police began descending on the small war being waged, with Katie sitting in the passenger seat of the police captain's car. As they approached, they saw Pagan land a punch flush in the jaw of Jayden, sending him into a newsstand. James picked up a crashed motorcycle and swung it at Drake. Drake jumped back, watching as the motorcycle missed him but connected with the back of Pagan's head. Pagan went crashing into a large crowd of tourists. Pagan could feel the bones of the tourists break under his massive weight. People were screaming in pain and panic. Pagan shook the cobwebs from his head. As he stood to get back into the fight, he saw that he had crushed a woman with a stroller. He picked up the stroller and lifted the crying baby from the stroller. Smiling an evil grin he carried the baby by the back of his overalls back into the street.

There was pandemonium on the strip. Traffic was backed up for miles. Cars were overturned, and sirens could be heard in every direction. As usual, the mob of people was not smart enough to leave the area entirely and wanted to watch the action from up close. Many of them had paid the price with their lives.

Katie stepped out of the cop car and ran into the melee. The police officer grabbed his bullhorn, barking out instructions to the vampires, who let his commands fall on deaf ears. Jayden and Drake were now circling each other. James, Aaliyah, and Katie stood across from Pagan, who held the baby in front of him. Suddenly a pair of blurs passed them, and the police captain went flying into the air. Then the police car was lifted into the air and hurled at James. James was hit square in the chest and went sprawling back across the street. The girls had to dive out of the way to avoid the impact.

Pagan threw the baby into the air toward the lake. Aaliyah sprinted toward the baby and dove, catching it curling around it just before it hit the water. During the confusion, Katie was caught off guard, and Pagan grabbed her into a choke from behind. The blur passed again and smashed the remaining five police cars and their inhabitants. A news helicopter appeared above them, as did a police chopper. One of the blurs finally stopped. It was Tariq. He ripped the door off of the ruins of a police car and hurled it into the sky, hitting the news helicopter. The helicopter went into a flat spin and crashed into the police helicopter. Both helicopters crashed into the adjacent resorts, causing a monstrous explosion and wide spread panic.

The news crews were not able capture the vampires on camera as they were forced to remain behind traffic and vehicle pile-ups. The few people with cameras were unable to get clear shots of the people involved, as they moved too quickly.

Drake jumped on the hood of an adjacent car and pushed off to kick Jayden in the face. Jayden felt his jaw crack, and moments later he felt it begin to heal. Drake threw another hard punch, only this time Jayden slipped the punch, grabbed Drake, and tossed him with all his might at Tariq. Tariq and Drake tumbled over each other on the asphalt. As Jayden sprinted to jump on his downed opponent, Kristoff suddenly re-entered the picture. He pounced on Drake, so Jayden jumped on Tariq. Both Jayden and Tariq were landing vicious punches from the top.

Jayden was becoming a blur of strikes. Tariq was unable to heal due to the constant onslaught. Jayden raised his fist to deliver the deathblow when he was hit from the side with extreme force and knocked twenty feet from Tariq. He couldn't see who had hit him. He and the vampire who hit him began throwing blind punches from the ground. As they skidded to a stop the other vampire had the top position, and for the first time Jayden and his brother stared into each other's immortal eyes.

Pagan yelled at Kristoff; standing behind Katie, he held her by the throat. Kristoff had knocked Drake unconscious and finally turned to address Pagan. Leaving Tariq and Pagan lying on the pavement, he advanced on Pagan.

"No closer, old man, or I promise I will break her neck," Pagan threatened.

"Let her go or I will kill your master, Pagan" Kristoff threatened as he stepped backward onto Drake's neck.

Neither man flinched. Both felt they had the upper hand. This was the only still moment since the fight began.

James dusted himself off and rubbed his cracked ribs as they healed themselves. He pulled himself from the police car debris, and found himself behind Pagan and Katie. Pagan held her captive and was talking to Kristoff. James raged as quietly as he could and sprang.

Pagan dug his nails into the girl's neck. This was almost too easy, he thought. As soon as Drake and Tariq healed they would outmatch Kristoff, and his coven's newest member, Stephan, was keeping Jayden indisposed.

Pagan suddenly felt a large pair of fangs dig into his throat, blood spilling everywhere. His fingernails tightened around Katie's throat. The more James ripped at his throat, the deeper his nails went into Katie's helpless neck. Her blood began to flow, mixing with his on the ground. Pagan grabbed a silver switchblade he kept in his pocket and plunged it into Katie's chest, just missing her heart. He broke the blade off and let her fall to the earth. Then with the last of his energy, he pulled James's fangs free of his neck and tossed him to the ground.

Still standing on Drake's neck, Kristoff lifted Tariq into the air by the collar. Tariq was starting to heal but was not strong enough yet to thwart off Kristoff.

"I thought you defended the weak? I thought you didn't believe in the mass executions anymore?" Kristoff asked.

Tariq lay limp in Kristoff's grip.

"Let them go," Stephan's voice rang out.

Stephan walked beside his brother up to Kristoff.

"He means let Tariq go," Jayden said. "I want to finish Drake."

"No, I mean let them both go," Stephan said.

"These men are brothers; you know what that means, Jayden. If you kill Drake, Tariq will hunt you down … and so will I. I won't have a choice."

"You always have a choice, Stephan. Drake killed my daughter and son. I'm taking him out. Do not get in my way."

"You know I can't fight an order from my master. Why would you force me to do this? Would you kill your own brother to get vengeance for your children?"

Jayden narrowed his eyes and stared at his younger brother. Letting his fangs lowers he hissed, "Yes."

Dripping wet, Aaliyah came running over.

"*Stop!*" She bent down at Katie's side and picked her daughter up.

"My baby is dying, Jayden!" Crying uncontrollably, she looked at Kristoff.

"Why isn't she healing?"

Kristoff looked at Pagan, who tossed the broken switchblade at his feet.

"She has silver lodged in her chest keeping her from healing fully. I'd say she has three days tops. There is only one person I know who might be able to save her … Vladimir. I can take her to him, but I cannot guarantee anything."

"We're coming with you," Aaliyah stammered

"Unfortunately, I cannot allow you to take that risk. Vladimir is unpredictable. He has killed hundreds of vampires throughout his lifetime. He has no incentive to not kill you," Kristoff retorted.

"He has reason to save Katie as she is the last living in his bloodline,"

Jayden walked toward Drake during this dialogue and grabbed him by the neck and leaned in so they were inches apart.

"You will die by my hand, you son of a bitch," Jayden growled. He tossed him back, and Drake landed on his feet, his balance returning. Drake smiled back at him, his missing teeth growing back.

"Well then I'll see you soon, sweetie," Drake said.

"Not if I see you first," Jayden responded.

Stephan picked Tariq up from the pavement, gingerly dusting him off.

"The sun is coming, Jay, get Katie where she needs to go. I love you bro. So please don't come after us, and I will try to keep these guys away from you." Stephan said.

"What? You aren't coming with us!" Jayden exclaimed.

"I have my family in you Jay, but my coven is here with Tariq."

Stephan stepped toward his brother with his arms out. Jayden tentatively hugged his brother. As they ended the embrace, Jayden grabbed his brother's arm.

"Until Drake is dead, you are dead to me."

He released Stephan's arm, and the two covens rushed away to avoid the morning sun.

The family headed toward the private airport with blinding speed. Jayden carried his daughter, who could not stop bleeding. Kristoff glamoured the pilot of the G-5 Jet, while James shut all the window shades in the cabin. In twenty minutes, the plane was leaving the runway destined for Vladimir's mountain.

Chapter 36

Jayden, Aaliyah, and James returned to the Endsley house. They all slept the day away. When they awoke that evening they checked their voicemail to see if there was any update from Kristoff. There was no message from him, but there was a message on James's phone from the hospital saying his father had no signs of improvement and was still in the ICU. The three of them decided to drive to the hospital.

Sitting in the front passenger seat Aaliyah asked Jayden, "What did you think when you saw Stephan?"

"I don't know. I wish I had turned him when I had the chance."

"Are you really ready to kill him if it comes to it?" she asked.

"I know there is a great moral lesson I should learn here about Vengeance. They say he who kills for revenge should dig two graves. I agree. One for Drake and one for anyone who stands in my way ... including Stephan."

James spoke up from behind, "Please turn up the radio; I think it's about us."

It came on. *"In what some have dubbed Halloween Havoc, the terrorist attack on the strip has caused more than nine hundred and fifty confirmed deaths and caused an estimated two hundred million dollars in damage, with an unknown amount in tourism being affected. There have been at least one hundred eyewitness reports with many different stories of what happened. Some say the terrorists were wearing vampire masks, while others say they were lobbing grenades at each other. This calculated combined attack utilized rocket propelled grenades to shoot down police and news helicopters, sources say. No domestic terrorist group has taken responsibility, and no Jihadist websites have claimed responsibility either. We will keep you informed as events unfold. "*

The foursome entered the hospital and walked to the ICU. They walked through the maze of hallways following Ronin's scent. When they arrived at his room, they entered to see him with tons of needles and sensors connected to his body. James stepped to his father's side. Grabbing his dad's hand, avoiding the needle driven through the back of it, James knelt beside the bed. Ronin's bloodshot eyes opened to see his son. He struggled to speak with the intubation tube down his throat. He pulled it out slowly, causing himself to gag. He turned his head to face his son.

"Lookin good, kid," he croaked. "Thanks for getting me out of there. I didn't want to die there. I'm much happier dying with you by my side."

"Dad you're going to get better, because I need you." James cried into his dad's hand. The blood tears began flowing uncontrollably from James.

"No, son, this is it for me. I've fought as hard as I can, and the doctors say it doesn't look good for me."

Jayden and Aaliyah looked at each other. Jayden walked to his best friend's side. "I love you, big man.

And I can't let you leave this world, us, or your son." Ronin looked up at Jayden. "And I can't let him become consumed with the same vengeance I am."

"Well unless you have some degree in medicine I am unfamiliar with, I'm done, bro," Ronin cried.

Jayden let his fangs descend, "I might know a trick or two."

Epilogue

Martin Harper stepped through the halls of the pentagon with an attaché case handcuffed to his wrist. Stepping through door after door, he finally arrived in a dimly lit room with a projector screen and a long mahogany table. Seated at the table were twelve of the most powerful generals in the US military. Mr. Harper uncuffed the case from himself. He pulled out twelve folders marked Top Secret and passed them out. He loaded a memory stick into the computer and addressed the generals. After briefing them on the bizarre mission in Iraq where they lost one soldier and had one go missing, the generals sat stone-faced. They all pored through the file, and finally the general sitting at the head of the table asked, "Is this for real?"

"Take a look for yourself sir"

Mr. Harper pressed play on the projector, and suddenly a black and white video started it showed Stephan following Sergeant Ford into the roofless house. As the video continued, many of the generals cringed. But the head general simply smiled and stated, "Ladies and Gentlemen, it looks like we have a new target.

www.ingramcontent.com/pod-product-compliance
Lightning Source LLC
Chambersburg PA
CBHW070550130626
46556CB00001B/89